The Truth Can Get You Killed

Mark Richard Zubro

St. Martin's Press
New York

Library of Congress Cataloging-in-Publication Data

Zubro, Mark Richard.
The truth can get you killed / by Mark Richard Zubro.
—1st ed.
p. cm.
ISBN 0-312-15679-0
1. Turner, Paul (Fictitious character)—Fiction. I. Title.
PS3576.U225T78 1997
813'.54—dc21 97-2490
CIP

First Edition: August 1997

10 9 8 7 6 5 4 3 2 1

To my nephews and nieces:
Adam, Heather, John, Leslie, and Rebecca

Acknowledgments

For their kind help and assistance:
Barb D'Amato, Rick Paul, Kathy Pakieser-Reed,
and Paul Varnell

The Truth Can Get You Killed

1

Dancing on top of the bar, the nearly naked man smiled and winked at Paul Turner. The Chicago police detective gave him an indifferent nod. Brushing past Turner, a heavy-set gentleman in his late fifties bellied up to the three-foot by five-foot stage and held a dollar out to the dancer. The nubile young thing, who wore only a black leather thong, swiveled his hips seductively as he bent down to receive the dollar and plant a kiss on the man's bald pate. Payment given and received, the presumably-over-twenty-one young man resumed his gyrations, now slinking toward another man with a dollar in his hand and a prominent bulge in his pants.

The New Year's Eve party at Au Naturel, the hottest gay bar in Chicago, was in full swing. Men, and a few women, crammed themselves together, elbow to elbow, watching the dancer, shouting at their friends over the retro-disco sound track, or quaffing tankards of beer—the specialty of the house, not counting the dancers.

After Paul checked his coat, it took him nearly ten minutes to work his way through the throng to reach the back bar where he'd promised to meet Ian and Ben. He found Ian Hume first. It was hard to miss his six-foot-six friend and his slouch fedora. Ian only took off the hat for meals and when he slept. Paul's friend and former lover was nuzzling the ear of a man in his early twenties. Paul guessed Ian's buddy was one of the dancers. Most everyone else wore sweaters, jeans, and other accoutrements against the ten-below-zero temperature outside. The young person with Ian's tongue in his ear was wearing only a flaming red and Day-Glo green kilt.

Paul nudged Ian's arm. Ian ignored the movement and swung his hip further into the young man's crotch. Paul jostled him more emphatically. Ian's look of exasperation turned to pleasure when he caught sight of Paul.

"You made a new friend," Paul said. In the back bar, it wasn't necessary to shout to be heard but you did have to raise your voice.

"Put enough dollar bills in his G-string and he'll be your friend, too."

"Where's Ben?"

"Sulking in a corner somewhere."

"Ben doesn't sulk."

Ian shrugged. "He was talking to Myra last I saw him."

Years ago, Ian and Paul had been lovers and they'd remained close friends. Under the rubric of honesty, Ian often felt compelled to announce his feelings about Paul's boyfriends. It wasn't that Ian necessarily disliked Ben Vargas, but their relationship was coolly neutral.

Paul gazed around at the raucous crowd. This section of Au Naturel was set up around an immense mahogany oval bar. They redecorated the walls every six months. This season's motif was scenes of Olympic athletes. Someone had taken newspaper photos and blown them up to half life size. Whether the original pictures were erotic by accident or design, the effect now was sensuous and inviting.

Clustered against the walls were high tables about a foot in diameter with tall bar stools nestled around them. Tonight, people clumped tightly around these and overflowed from them, completely filling the normally spacious room. A few patrons watched forty-eight-inch television screens filled with scenes of revelers in various cities around the country waiting outdoors for midnight. High on the walls, smaller screens continuously showed music videos of groups Paul had never heard of.

Paul tried to get the bartender's attention but that frazzled personage was juggling three large tankards. Paul held out a ten dollar bill high in the air over the bar and, even then, it took over five minutes to be noticed. Tonight more than usual, Paul suspected they watered the drinks—despite the outsized drinking vessels favored by Au Naturel. Finally fortified, Paul began a circuit of the room.

He found Ben and Myra huddled in a corner. Ben gave him a wan smile. Myra frowned. She pushed through a couple who were either trying to dance very close together or in the middle of foreplay.

Myra glared at him and leaned toward his ear. "Are you all right?"

"Yes."

"You should have called," she said.

"I tried to."

"You better talk to him."

Paul sighed. He eased next to Ben. He put his tankard of beer on the floor up against the wall. He gave him a hug, which Ben barely returned.

"What's wrong?" Paul asked.

"I've been worried," Ben said. "Are you all right?"

"Yes."

"You should have called."

"I did. I got you the new answering machine for Christmas."

"I haven't had time to hook it up."

"And I left messages at the shop."

"When?"

"I tried to get you before you left."

When Ben spoke his deep voice had an uncharacteristic tremor. His eyes didn't waver from Paul's as he explained. "George runs into the body shop at one this afternoon. He's all out of breath. He says that two detectives from Area Ten have been shot. I drop everything and rush to the television.

All I see is live coverage of one ambulance pulling away and a helicopter landing to pick up the other victim. I can't see the person. The reporter can't or won't say who it is or how badly they're hurt. I don't know if it's you, if you've been hurt, or if you're dead. I call Area Ten. You aren't there, but no one will tell me where you are. I heard the guy I was talking to snicker. He didn't even bother to cover the receiver when he said to somebody, 'The faggot's boyfriend is on the phone.' I run down to Mrs. Talucci's to get her to place the call. She's watching the same live coverage. She tells me to calm down. How can I? She places the call. The line is busy for the next hour. I tried calling Madge Fenwick. She would have been able to call Fenwick's beeper. She wasn't home. I'm crazy with worry. Mrs. Talucci promises to keep trying. I go back to work. I've even more frustrated because I have to have intermediaries call. Sure you don't get hassled much about being gay, but it still isn't the same. I can't call like other people's husbands or wives and ask the same kinds of questions."

Paul kept his eyes focused on Ben's as his lover spoke. Their faces were inches apart so Ben didn't have to shout to be heard.

"I'm sorry," Paul said. "Buck and I were on the north side of the city hunting through some debris in an arson murder case that had connections to one of ours down here. No one contacted me."

Ben interrupted. "See, it does make a difference that you're gay."

"They didn't get hold of Buck either."

"That was probably deliberate, too."

That was too paranoid for Paul to respond to. He understood that his companion of over two years was worried. Anybody in a relationship with a cop had to face the problem of anxiety about the dangers their loved one might encounter on the job.

"Ben, I didn't find out about the shooting until I got back to Area Ten around five. They already had the suspects in jail."

"Somebody could have had the decency to tell you I called."

"Madge heard it on her car radio and came down to the station."

"Is that what you want me to do, come down to the station?"

For all the implications this had about Paul being gay, a cop, and mildly open at work, he answered. "That would be okay. I don't want you to worry."

Ben frowned. "If I came to Headquarters, you could get hassled."

"I could get a pager like Buck's."

"Might help."

"Or we could set up a system where Madge calls you?"

"So I can be a second-class citizen? Heterosexuals can call but I can't?"

"Come on, Ben, be reasonable. After Madge showed up at the station, I realized you might worry. I tried calling. You weren't home. I called Mrs. Talucci but she had left for a New Year's Eve dinner with some friends in Wicker Park. The shop was closed. I tried calling."

"I promised to see my parents for a while. Dad still gets upset if I don't stop by."

Four months ago, Ben's father had a mild stroke. His mother could mostly manage his dad, but the older man insisted that his son visit frequently. This was a major strain on Ben's time but he didn't feel he could say no to his ailing dad.

Paul said, "I had to stop at Jeff's sleep-over. It's a big deal for him. It is for me, too. Parents had to be there by seven and leave by nine. I told you all this."

"I know," Ben said. "I wish I felt more reasonable. I wish our schedules weren't so hectic, but I was scared." He wiped his eyes with his sleeve, took a deep breath, and then continued, "Before I left for here, I finally tried Madge again. She told me you were both okay. I went through pure hell today. Lately, I get frightened every time you leave. I don't know if it's the last time I'm ever going to see you."

Being the wife, husband, or lover of a cop often wasn't easy.

A high rate of alcoholism, suicide, and divorce came with a job the dangers of which, while statistically remote, were still very real. Most officers never pulled their guns in their entire careers, but that didn't stop the worry and anxiety among loved ones and the cops themselves.

"I tried to call," Paul said. "I love you. I'm sorry that you were worried. I wish you wouldn't. It doesn't help anything to worry."

"That's what you always say."

Paul took Ben in his arms. He felt the well-muscled body against his own. He rubbed his hands over the broad shoulders. "I'm sorry," he said. "I love you. I'm sorry."

He felt Ben's muscles relax, tension easing. Ben's head nestled into the crook of Paul's neck and shoulder. His arms pulled Paul close.

The subject both of them ignored was that of Paul quitting his job. Ben had broached the subject once and it had led to one of the most difficult times in their relationship. As gently as he could, Paul had made it clear that he would not give up being a detective. At the time, they had talked for hours but come no closer to a solution. Like other couples, they had to hope that love and closeness and caring would get them over the rough spots.

Paul shut his eyes. He took little note of the annoying background noise and the occasional jostling. He felt Ben's cheek against this own. Ben's lips nuzzled into his hair. Paul liked being coupled. He loved Ben. He was briefly annoyed that he'd let Ian talk them into going out on one of the craziest nights of the year. Then he felt Ben's hip shift into his groin. He maneuvered the front of his pants to match Ben's.

Myra returned with three fresh tankards of ale. Paul and Ben unclinched but kept their arms around each other. She looked at Ben. "Everything better?" she asked him.

He nodded.

She glanced down at the front of his pants. "I can see they

are." She gave each of them a playful punch on the bicep. "You guys are such studs. If I were a man, I'd find both of you hot." She smiled at them and passed the tankards around.

"Where's the woman of the hour?" Paul asked.

Myra's latest beau had been expected to meet them here tonight. Six months ago, Myra's lover of five years had taken off for the mountains of northern California with an encyclopedia saleswoman from Muncie, Indiana. Myra said, "The bitch called and left a message on my answering machine. Said she was going to 'blow off our date.' No reason. No explanation. I heard party noises in the background. She's probably drunk and whining in somebody's ear. Good riddance."

Myra had a penchant for dating extremely dependent, alcoholic ex-nuns.

Ian, without a dancer attached, joined them.

"Where's the man of the moment?" Paul asked.

"Dancing."

"With what you shell out, I wouldn't think he'd need to."

"I'm willing to share. What I shell out is in return for services rendered."

"I believe the technical term for that is prostitution," Paul said.

"He'll go home with me without my having to pay."

Myra said, "I've got ten bucks that says that's a crock. Anybody else?"

Ian took the bet. Paul and Ben added ten each of their own.

Ian said to Paul, "Speaking of money, tonight are you going to reward any of the dancers with a monetary gift?"

"I might," Paul said.

"You say that, and you never do."

"When I'm here, do you watch me every minute?"

Ben said, "There was this humpy number with a hairy chest and big pecs he donated several dollars to last time."

Paul put his arm around Ben's shoulder, "I like hairy chested men with tight muscles."

"Well, grand," Ian said, "but if I remember right, the last time you were here was in June after the Pride Parade. If I see one of your type tonight, I'll send him over."

"You can keep him," Paul said.

Ian fended his way through the mass of people to the bar for another drink.

Paul and Ben drove home a little after midnight. Paul had to be to work by eight the next morning. They left Ian attached to his new friend, and Myra attempting to seduce a librarian from Kankakee.

Back at his house, Paul led the way upstairs. It was rare that they had the place to themselves. Paul couldn't stay overnight at Ben's, because he had to be home for his sons. This New Year's, however, Jeff was at the indoor camp-out. The gym at Sheridan Park, two blocks away, had been rented out for the night and most of the next day for special needs kids. They would put up tents on the basketball court, play games, sit around an electric campfire, and sing songs. For wheelchair-bound kids for whom the outdoors could pose insurmountable obstacles, this was a real treat. It also gave the parents a night away from the constant responsibilities inherent in having a child with special needs.

Paul's older son, Brian, a senior in high school, was in Miami for the Orange Bowl. Brian and his friend Jose had been named to the Illinois High School all-state football team. As a reward they were given tickets to the Orange Bowl and the NFL play-off game the next day. The school's band was scheduled to march in the Orange Bowl parade, so there were school personnel available for chaperoning. Brian had worked evenings and weekends at Ben's garage to pay for his half of the room and his plane fare.

Paul had talked to the exuberant Brian several times in the past few days. Paul had worried slightly about not going along, but getting out of work over the holidays, for a cop, was tough. Leaving Jeff was not possible. Taking him along would have been fine, but Jeff's heart was set on being with his friends at the sleep-over. Paul didn't want to favor one boy over the other, and he knew the coach and chaperones going to Miami. He was as certain as any parent could be that there wouldn't be any problems.

As soon as he closed the front door, Paul grabbed Ben and pulled him close. As they kissed, hats, coats, gloves, and scarves cascaded to the floor. At the first pause for breath, Paul said, "It's great to know it's just the two of us." Ben had been sleeping over almost continuously of late. Paul felt extremely comfortable with this.

When they arrived upstairs in the bedroom, Paul stopped Ben from taking off the rest of his clothes. Silently, Paul helped Ben shed his sweater and then began slowly unbuttoning his lover's shirt.

"I'm sorry I got so worried," Ben said. "I'll try to be less paranoid."

"To have someone who cares so much is a rare and precious thing. I wouldn't want to lose it. I promise to get a pager."

"I guess that'll help."

Paul continued, "I want to do whatever I can to help you worry less. Pagers aren't a perfect solution, but I'll get one."

Paul pulled the tails of the opened shirt out of Ben's pants. He caressed the deep growth of fur on Ben's chest. Paul opened the closet door and selected a metal-studded leather belt. He gently rubbed the tip over Ben's torso. His lover groaned. Paul eased his lover's pants and white briefs down a few inches and fastened the belt around Ben's waist.

Ben drew a deep breath as Paul's lips nuzzled their way from the belt buckle to his neck. Their lips met and their bodies strained close together.

2

The watch commander marched up to Paul Turner and Buck Fenwick as they strolled into the squad room the next morning. He said, "You guys got a call about a dead body in a dumpster up on an alley off Lincoln Avenue."

"And Happy New Year to you," Fenwick said.

"Just as dead today as any other day." The watch commander gave them the address and then stalked away.

"Must have had a rough New Year's," Fenwick said.

"Did I miss something," Turner said, "or hasn't he been unpleasant since he got assigned here five months ago?"

"Been an asshole for a while. Latest I heard about him is that he made it so tough for some guys up in the Fourteenth District that they were thinking of filing suit against him."

"Being an asshole is now an actionable offense? The courts could never handle all the cases."

"If they put me in charge, it wouldn't be a problem. I'd just have them executed." Fenwick felt the death penalty was okay as long as he got to pick out who was executed and for what offenses. He often threatened to start with the pitching staff of the Chicago Cubs. His frequently expressed opinion was that, if the pitchers on the team knew that the first one to walk a batter every year would be summarily shot, the team would have a chance of winning a pennant. Turner doubted this.

As they walked through Area Ten Headquarters, they maneuvered around numerous homeless people allowed to huddle in various corners of the station overnight for warmth. The mass of people added to the smell and confusion of the overflow crowd of drunks and out-of-control party-goers whom Chicago's cops had deemed unworthy or unable to find their own way home last night.

They signed out a car and Fenwick drove through the nearly deserted streets with his usual kamikaze flair. Patches of ice and fifteen-below-zero temperatures wouldn't put a dent in Fenwick's urge to careen madly through the streets. Today Fenwick included banging on the controls of the car's heating unit to his driving drill. It took several minutes for the thin trickle of heat to ooze from the car vents. At first, Buck fiddled with the controls at every stop, then he'd started banging with the flat of his hand.

Before Fenwick could totally destroy the dashboard, Turner took a stab at coaxing enough puffs of heat from the engine to keep the cold at bay. His calm manipulations did little more than Fenwick's bashing.

Area Ten ran from Fullerton Avenue on the north to Lake Michigan on the east, south to Fifty-ninth Street, and west to Halsted. It included the wealth of downtown Chicago and North Michigan Avenue, some of the nastiest slums in the city, along with numerous upscale developments. It incorporated four police districts. The cops in the Areas in Chicago handled homicides and any major nonlethal violent crimes. The Districts mostly took care of neighborhood patrols and initial responses to incidents. Turner had long since stopped correcting visitors who called where he worked a police precinct. One quick way to tell a crime victim/tourist from New York, or an incredibly stupid copyeditor, was their insistence on going to the precinct to report a crime.

Halfway to the murder scene, Paul mentioned his discussion last night with Ben. He finished, "I don't know who he got hold of at Area Ten."

"More than enough assholes in the place to pull that kind of stunt. I could snoop around."

"Let me think about that."

"Want me to have Madge talk to Ben?"

"It might help, but I'm not sure. A big part of the problem is that somebody blew him off because they assumed he was my lover. I doubt if Madge can fix that."

"Maybe just to reassure him. Madge has a way about her."

"The goofy thing is, how did the person who took the call know it wasn't just a friend or maybe a brother or even my dad?"

"Good question. Although even assholes can jump to conclusions."

These days Paul did not hide his sexuality from those with whom he worked closely. He figured part of the reason he hadn't had major problems with prejudice was that he'd worked in Area Ten for more than eleven years before his orientation became generally known. Since his wife's death, his natural reticence to talk about his private life left their speculations free to roam. Also, with lack of evidence to the contrary, people usually assumed you were straight.

Radical gay people might call this selling out, but it was a way a lot of gay people were out on the job. In the still predominantly straight male world of most, if not all, police departments, being an openly gay recruit left you vulnerable to harassment from your peers. Prejudice might be against the law, recruitment of gay officers a desired goal, but in the real world lots of young, straight, male cop wannabees could be vicious.

They pulled into the alley off Lincoln Avenue a block and a half south of Fullerton. They parked behind a blue-and-white squad car.

A clump of five people huddled under the eaves of a garage ten feet away. A few glanced in their direction. All of them, including Turner and Fenwick, wore heavy shoes, shirts, pants, socks, and coats. In the fifteen-below-zero temperatures, hats covered heads to well below the ears and scarves enwrapped mouths and faces. The fierce north wind dispersed the clouds of vapor formed by their breaths. Turner saw icicles building on the outside of the scarves where the steam escaped nearest the mouth.

"What have we got?" Turner asked.

A figure pointed ten feet away to a dark green garbage container. "Dead body in that dumpster. Bullet hole in the middle of his forehead. Trail of blood leads off in that direction." He aimed a glove at the far side of the dumpster. "Followed it, but it ends in the middle of the alley. Don't know if it'll help."

Turner didn't recognize any of the well-muffled faces, but he thought this voice was that of David McWilliams, a patrolman they'd worked with before.

"Who found the body?" Turner asked.

"I did," said the smallest of the muffled figures.

"You live around here?"

The person pointed to a house on the other side of the alley.

Turner said to McWilliams, "Why don't you take him in to where it's warm, and we'll check in with you later?"

McWilliams agreed with alacrity.

When the civilian was gone Fenwick asked, "This one in the pool?"

The detectives at Area Ten had placed bets on the time of the finding of the first dead body of the year in the part of the city they patrolled. They'd given up using the instant of death as the basis for their wagers, since that science was too inexact—the time the first call came in to the dispatcher was the key. Also the dead person had to have been murdered.

"Call came in at seven forty-seven."

"Got to be somebody earlier," Fenwick said. "I've got fifty bucks on two twenty-six."

The two detectives assigned a couple of the beat cops to

begin the canvass of the neighborhood. Another one was told to keep spectators away from the crime scene. This poor cop could keep warm in the patrol car, but would need to make forays into the alley if any brave but frozen local denizens appeared.

Turner gazed around the alley. It was completely deserted. Along the east side was a block of houses. On the west were the backs of businesses that fronted on Lincoln Avenue. He wasn't sure which business was which, but one of those nearby had to be the back door of Au Naturel. All the businesses and most of the homes abutted directly on each other. A few of the homes had a few feet between them. Most were unprepossessing, but Turner knew the average price of a home in this neighborhood was around $300,000. Lincoln Park was one of the most desirable areas in the city in which to live. Used-home buyers in this area often paid the high price, left the walls up for tax purposes, gutted the insides, and redid the whole interior, giving them a renovated home with an asking price of over $500,000.

The alley had been cleared of snow, as had most of the streets. A few inches of wind-driven ice crystals had fallen last week before the deep freeze hit. The scattered patches of snow were trodden well beyond the point of possibly holding any useful footprints. The frozen puddles of sparkling ice would be useless in providing any kind of clues.

Turner and Fenwick did not rush to see the body. They clutched pencils awkwardly in gloved hands as they made quick sketches of all they could see. Despite being well bundled against the cold, the wind seemed to seep between the threads of their clothing and brush their skin with icy trickles. Turner and Fenwick retired to the feeble warmth of the car to make more elaborate drawings and fill in what they'd started out in the cold. They left the car only when the Crime Lab truck pulled up behind their vehicle.

Fenwick, Turner, and two of the technicians slowly approached the dumpster. Five feet from the garbage coffin, they all stopped. An obvious trail of blood led from the side of the dumpster and then north down the alley.

After photos had been taken, Fenwick and Turner finally made a careful examination of the contents of the overgrown trash can. As they had been told, a body lay there with a bullet hole in the middle of the forehead. The hole was massive, attesting to a large-caliber fire arm. The detritus in the dumpster filled it about halfway. Every bit of garbage would have to be preserved. At least in its frozen state it wouldn't be as odiferous or offensive as it would be were it high summer in Chicago.

Fenwick touched the body. Frozen so stiff it might as well have been chipped from marble.

The investigation was slowed by the fact that every ten minutes, they retired to the Crime Lab van to get warm. As Fenwick put it, "I'm in no hurry to freeze to death, and the dead body isn't going to care."

The dead person was a white male who looked to be anywhere from his midfifties to midsixties. Weight probably around two hundred. Probably at least five-eight, although it was difficult to tell because the body was slightly twisted and scrunched up. Bald with a fringe of gray hair, large mole on the right ear, and clean shaven. He was wearing a navy blue overcoat over an Armani three-piece suit, and Gucci shoes.

They followed the trail of blood but, as they'd been told, it ended about ten feet down the alley. There was no indication where it might have gone from there or why it stopped. They'd have uniformed cops check the backyards and fronts of every building in this and the surrounding blocks.

After a thorough preliminary examination, Fenwick managed to free a billfold from the inside pocket of the man's overcoat. In the van, he and Turner examined the contents.

"Judge Albert Meade," Turner read.

"A judgesicle," Fenwick opined.

The name meant nothing to either of them. They knew many of the judges from the local criminal courts and this was not one of them. They found cards and identification for VISA and Mastercard, the Chicago Public Library, ATM, social security, voters registration, health and car insurance, along with sixty-one dollars. In the other pockets they had found car keys, three quarters, a dime, and a handkerchief.

In the van, Turner and Fenwick, the medical examiner, and the Crime Lab technicians gathered to discuss their findings.

"Definitely not robbery," Fenwick said.

Nods of agreement.

"He killed here?" Turner asked.

"Unlikely. Couple considerations. That wound would have bled a lot and there are no remnants of the bullet's exit. Blood trail stops so abruptly. Not sure it really says much about where the killer came from, but it says to me the dead guy was probably driven here. Of course, the killer could have been walking for any distance, body shifts, or moves, blood starts to drip. Or killer accidentally gets blood on his heel, any number of possibilities."

"Could the blood be the killer's and not the victim's?"

"Possible. After we've had it tested, we'll be able to tell."

"Could he have carried him from one of the houses nearby?"

"Sure, but why risk being seen?"

Fenwick said, "Duh, because where he shot him would have told us who the killer is?"

"Fenwick, how many killers has your sarcasm caught?" The question came from one of the old timers in the Medical Examiner's office.

"Two just last week," Fenwick retorted.

"Can we get on with it?" one of the Crime Lab people asked. "I want to see the kick-off of the Cotton Bowl."

"I don't think it was much of a risk either way," Turner said. "Driving up with or dragging around a body. No alley in

Chicago is going to have herds of people thundering down it at night. Cold as it was this morning, the killer could have thrown himself a party out here and not be noticed."

"Already started the canvass of the neighborhood."

"So, we're mostly agreed. Not killed here and was driven or carried to this spot."

"If the killer's going to put him in the dumpster, why stop the car ten feet away?"

"Maybe he didn't drive up."

"Or why not leave him in a dumpster closer to where the blood trail starts?"

"This is about halfway down the alley. Farthest from either street."

"Why not just leave him in the alley instead of toting him all the way to the dumpster and heaving him in?"

Universal shrugs.

"Then we've got a big criminal."

"Or at least a strong one."

"Dead guy's clothes are drenched with blood. Killer must have gotten it all over."

"With half his brain missing, we can rule out suicide."

Fenwick said, "Your perception of the obvious is remarkable."

"Somebody chain him outside in the cold."

Turner said, "Must have been killed somewhere else and brought here. Love to find out where."

Moving a victim from a crime scene was always a smart idea on the part of a criminal. Invariably, it made it tougher for the cops to solve a case. If you were going to get clues, the original crime scene would normally have the best ones. Some detectives swore that a killer always left their signature somewhere at the sight of the death.

One of the beat cops joined them. "Got the stuff you wanted on the guy. He was a federal judge in the Seventh Circuit, which includes all of Illinois and a couple surrounding states.

He's been on the bench twenty-three years and was a lawyer in town before then. He's got a wife and two kids. Lived in Chicago."

"Let's talk to our helpful citizen/body finder," Fenwick said. "No offense to you guys, but I want to get my ass into someplace totally warm."

3

Turner and Fenwick walked across the alley. They slowed their pace as they entered the yard. Each observed the path to the door and the surrounding area carefully. No sign of blood or of a body having been dragged or carried.

"You know what I hate most about winter?" Fenwick asked as they knocked on the back door of a Queen Anne–style house.

"Snow and cold?"

"That too." Fenwick pulled at the crotch of his pants, "No, my long winter underwear gives me jock itch."

"Thanks for sharing."

A now recognizable Dave McWilliams opened the back door of the house.

"He's in the kitchen," McWilliams told them.

Turner stopped for a minute and let the warmth of the home ease into his psyche. Jumping in and out of the cold had been miserable. He accepted a cup of coffee gratefully and let his hands surround the ceramic mug. He left his jacket on for the moment.

He glanced around the kitchen. The floors gleamed. The walls were done in very pale beige and the cabinets in a very muted, very light brown. A cuisinart in one corner. A microwave oven in another. Electric stove. Large refrigerator. Butcher-block table.

The beat cop donned his winter gear and left.

Calvin Hancock, whose home they were in, sat opposite Turner and Fenwick at the table. They thanked him for making the call and being helpful.

"Tell us how you happened to find the body," Fenwick said.

"I told the others already."

Hancock was around five-foot-two with spindly arms and a narrow pinched face. Turner didn't picture him toting around a two-hundred-pound corpse.

Neither loudly nor angrily, Fenwick said, "I don't like working on holidays when everybody else has off. I was going to miss three football games already today. Now, I'm going to miss at least seven because of this murder. I am not a very friendly person in general, so why don't you just tell us what happened without the crap, and we can all go home sooner?"

Hancock's eyes widened at Fenwick whose massive bulk took up a great deal of space in the reasonably large kitchen.

"I am home," Hancock said.

"Why don't you start at the beginning?" Fenwick suggested.

"Surely."

"Don't call me Shirley," Fenwick said.

Hancock looked as if he didn't know whether he should laugh at Fenwick's feeble humor or not.

Turner ignored Fenwick's crack. "Go ahead, Mr. Hancock."

The man gave a nineteenth-century upper-class British sniff. "Well, around seven this morning I took out the garbage from my party last night. Three of my friends and I have been getting together for dinner at one another's homes on New Year's Eve for twenty years. We don't like to be out on the streets or in crowded bars or at loud, uncivilized parties. One of us always cooks for the others. In the library, over coffee and dessert, we listened to Beethoven's Ninth Symphony. We always play that on New Year's. It's a memory of when we all went to college. We were so poor—it was the only album in the apartment, the first time we did this. I cleaned last night, but waited until I was going out for the papers today to take out the garbage.

This way I could combine the two trips. I didn't want to have to don all my winter accoutrements twice if I didn't have to."

"What happened in the alley?" Turner asked.

"My dumpster is across the way from the one with the body. I put my debris in my own and began to walk away. I noticed the red spots on the ground. At first I thought they were some kind of champagne or a sauce of some kind. The trail led to the dumpster opposite. The lid was open. I don't like that in our alley. Those businesses across the way don't watch for that as much as they should. Even in this weather leaving them open like that will attract vermin. I went over to close it. I reached for the lid and barely glanced in. As you know, the body was right there. I immediately returned here and phoned the police. I hope they still have some newspapers left when I'm finally allowed to go to the store."

"We're almost done, Mr. Hancock," Turner said.

"You know the dead guy?" Fenwick asked.

"Not from what I saw. I didn't look at the face that much. Who was it?"

"Albert Meade?"

"The judge?"

"You do know him?"

"I know of him. Every gay person who keeps up with the news should know who he is."

"Who is he?" Fenwick asked.

"Albert Meade is one of the three judges who ruled, the day before Christmas, that the antigay law in Du Page County was legal."

The name still meant nothing to Turner, but the upheld law did. Du Page County was immediately west of Chicago, known for its rock-ribbed Republicans, and legislators who were well in the running for first prize for being some of the most stupid, ignorant, and narrow-minded elected officials in the country. A year and a half ago the Du Page County Board had passed an ordinance forbidding any business or government body from treating gay people equally.

After the law was passed, outrage and protests had been followed by legal suits. As Hancock had said, the local federal circuit court had ruled last week on the side of the county. More furious protests had followed. Ian had let loose a tirade at their annual Christmas get-together about gays being second-class citizens ending with the declaration that he wasn't going to go quietly when they came to get him for the concentration camps.

Turner doubted if six people in the country could name more than a few of the Supreme Court justices much less those from lower courts in the circuits.

Calvin Hancock slowly stood up. "Judge Meade is dead! I found the body." He paused briefly and then an enormous smile crossed his face. "Thank god. I can't think of a dead person I'd rather speak evil of." The man almost capered around the room. "Wait until I tell everyone. I'll be a celebrity. I hope I'm on every talk show. Oprah, I'm ready for my close-up." Calvin hummed several bars of "Ding-dong the Witch Is Dead."

Turner understood the feeling. He wondered about the implications of him being gay and investigating the murder. Maybe he should dismiss himself from the case. He could never hope to be objective.

Fenwick said, "Mr. Hancock, I've never seen anyone happier to see someone dead."

Calvin smiled at them. "You think my being happy makes me a suspect?"

"The thought crossed my mind."

"Forget it. I'm a lawyer. I know precisely what I'm saying. If you're going to arrest everyone in the city, or even the country for that matter, who is happy about this piece of shit being dead, you'll have to haul in every faggot in three thousand miles and some in foreign countries, too."

"But you knew who he was after we said his name."

"I'm a lawyer and a gay activist. I follow all these cases carefully. I didn't file the brief in this instance, but I'm head of the local Gay Lawyers Guild. If my being happy he's dead is going to get brutality from the cops, I'm ready. I dare you to try anything with me. When they come to take me away in the middle of the night, I will not go quietly."

"Nobody's taking anybody to concentration camps," Fenwick said. "We're just trying to get some answers."

"And you got some. All you're going to get. I told you what happened. You want to know how I feel about him being dead? Like the Jews in the concentration camps must have felt when told that Hitler was dead. Every gay person you talk to will feel the same way."

When they got in the car and got the heater going as best they could, Fenwick asked, "Is that how you feel?"

"What?"

"Happy that he's dead."

"I don't have a history of knowing about him like Hancock did, but I'd be lying if I didn't think this was one less homophobic asshole on the planet. Hard for me not to be pleased about that."

"You gonna ask to be taken off the case?"

"Ethically, I don't think I have a choice."

"You take yourself off, you're going to have to do a lot of explaining. By now half the Area Ten personnel know that a prominent judge bought it in the city and that we got the case. People will want to know why you want off. If you don't say anything, they'll speculate. If you do tell, you risk repercussions. Commander Poindexter is probably okay and most of the detectives, but I don't know about this temporary commander we've got. Look what happened when Ben called. Whoever wouldn't help him yesterday is still working in the station. He almost certainly has friends who feel the same way."

"Being in or out of the closet, now or ever, is not going to make a difference in my being on a case or not."

Fenwick was quiet a minute then said, "Sorry."

"Forget it. I understand what you said, and it's all too possible. The main questions is how can I work on a murder case of someone I'm not sorry is dead? The killer probably deserves a medal."

"You can't quit the case. What if they assign me Carruthers as a partner?"

"Just shoot him and leave him in a dumpster. If someone bothers to report it, any cops would take one look and walk away."

Carruthers was the curse of the Area Ten day shift. He'd spent the week before Christmas with his wife and two kids in Hawaii. To the surprise of no one, he'd returned to work on Christmas Eve in a Day-Glo, flower-print shirt. Everyone had studiously ignored him.

"I wish the commander wasn't on vacation," Fenwick said. "He'd be all right with it. You can't just up and quit a case."

They located the local beat cop in charge of coordinating the neighborhood canvass. Turner and Fenwick asked about the status of the questioning.

They had gotten to about half of the neighbors, but to only a few of the businesses. Most of the latter were closed. Many of the bars would open in a few hours, especially ones with televisions tuned to the many football games of the day. No one interviewed so far had seen anything in the alley.

Turner and Fenwick walked quickly down the alley for two blocks south and then north for a block and a half where the large bulk of Children's Hospital prevented the alley from going through any farther in that direction. They also walked around the entire immediate block.

As they made their neighborhood survey, the day seemed to be getting colder not warmer. By the time they were done, even the feeble warmth of the car felt good.

4

They decided to visit the judge's wife first. The address they had from the beat cop was on Belle Plaine Avenue. This was a street in a small enclave of wealthy homes between Sheridan Road and Clarendon, just north of Irving Park Road.

The as yet unfrozen water of the lake steamed as they took the Drive north. They turned off on Irving Park, drove several blocks west to Sheridan, and took it north to Belle Plaine. The short street was lined with giant trees, bare of leaves, fronting mansions that would have done a stretch of southern plantations proud. This was a bright spot of gentility in a neighborhood generously referred to as eclectic. In a few years, the surrounding area of the city might be totally gentrified but, for the moment, it could have its dicier areas.

They walked up to the two-story, red-brick Regency house. The door was answered by a white-haired woman who looked, Turner guessed, to be in her late fifties. She wore gray pants and a pin-stripe coat over a white blouse.

Turner said, "Mrs. Meade?"

"Yes."

Turner introduced himself and Fenwick and showed his identification. "May we come in?" he asked. "We need to speak with you."

"Is something wrong?"

Turner wasn't about to give her tragic news while standing

in the doorway as a winter wind whipped off the lake and rushed the cold around them and into her house.

"Please, Mrs. Meade. I'm afraid I have bad news. If we could come in."

She looked from one to the other, frowned, then nodded, and held the door open for them to enter.

They set foot in a front hall with a highly polished hardwood floor. Directly in front of them, a red-carpeted stairway swept upward in a narrow curve. A highly polished suit of armor stood in the corner on their right. On their left was an Enfield cupboard in stained cherry. She brought them into a parlor on the left with a dark-brown-and-purple Persian rug, white walls, and black-leather furniture.

After they were seated, she asked, "What's wrong? Has something happened to my children?"

"No, ma'am," Turner said. "We have unfortunate news. Earlier today we found a man with your husband's identification. He was dead."

"Here, in Chicago?"

"Yes, ma'am."

"That's impossible. My husband is in Montreal at a convention of jurists."

Fenwick described the body.

When he finished, she held up a hand to her face. "I can't understand it," she said. "How can it be him?"

Turner showed her the driver's license and other identification from the wallet they had found.

"Someone must have stolen it from his wallet. Albert wouldn't lie to me. He's in Montreal. I'll call him." She bustled out of the room, returning moments later with a slip of paper in hand. She picked up the receiver and pressed in the numbers. When she hung up she said, "He never checked in."

As gently as they could, they got her to accompany them down to Cook County Morgue. The ride occurred in strained silence. Once there, the identification was brief and complete. She took one look, gasped, and burst into tears.

They led her down the hall to a quiet office. Upon entering she said, "I have to call the children." She sat in a green vinyl-covered chair. "How can I tell the children? What can I tell them? What happened?" She dabbed at her eyes with a tissue that Turner had provided from a nearby desk.

"Someone murdered him."

"Why?"

"That's what we need to find out," Turner said. "If we could ask you a few questions. The first hours of a case are important. You might be able to give us some information that could lead to the killer."

"I can't imagine I know anything. What happened to my husband? I don't know if I can talk."

"Please, Mrs. Meade, if you'd make the attempt. We'll help you call your children, or get someone to come down and assist you, but if you could answer a few questions, it might give us directions to pursue in the investigation."

Her nod of acquiescence was more numb shock than aware willingness to help.

"You said he was supposed to be in Montreal," Turner prompted.

"Yes, he left yesterday for the convention. He was scheduled to return Sunday."

"How was he planning to get there?"

"He had a seven o'clock flight out of O'Hare. He loved Montreal and was leaving a day early so he could enjoy some of his favorite sights."

"Who took him to the airport?"

"He rode the El. He always said it was silly to pay good money for a taxi or a limo or waste the time fighting traffic. It's less than two dollars. The El takes you right to the terminal. I don't know why I care about that right now. I'm a wreck and I'm confused and I'm frightened."

'Why are you frightened?" Fenwick asked.

"Because now I'm alone."

A general round of throat clearing and pausing occurred before Fenwick asked the next question. "You didn't see him get on the plane?"

"He went by himself."

"How did you know he was in Montreal?"

"When he's on a business trip, he usually calls when he gets in, but there were delays in Montreal. He called me from the airport here. For a while, he thought he might have to wait until tomorrow for a flight. He got the last one out. He wouldn't get into Montreal until after two in the morning, so he said he would call today. He never did."

"Did he have any unusual problems recently? Any sign of tension?"

"No, nothing. We'd had a good Christmas with the children. He said it was silly to go north in winter for a convention, but he was looking forward to it. He would see lots of old friends. It was a convention on international law. It was something he loved."

"Did he receive any threats recently, have any disagreements with people he worked with, any fights? Criminals he put in jail threatening him?"

"No, no. Nothing like that. Certainly nothing he told me about. He would have told me. We were happily married. He confided in me. We used to get a few threats after his pro-life rulings a while back, but we have an answering service, and our mail is screened. He hadn't received any threats in the past few years that I know about."

"Fights in the family or with co-workers?"

"Nothing like that."

"We'll need to speak to your children."

"Mike, our son, went back to school early. He's just turned twenty-two. Pam, our daughter, is on vacation in California. She's twenty-six."

They wrote down the address of the son and the name of the hotel the daughter was staying in.

"Where did you spend last night?" Fenwick asked.

"I went out to a restaurant for an early dinner with some

friends. They wanted me to go out to a party, but I came home early and read a book."

She called a friend to meet her at her house when she arrived. They arranged for one of the local beat cops to take her home. Turner and Fenwick walked with her out to the police car. As Turner held the door for her Fenwick said, "If you think of anything, please call us."

As she entered the car, she nodded distractedly at him. She tapped the young officer on the shoulder and murmured, "Take me home, please."

5

Turner insisted they detour to the Speedy Electronics store at Broadway and Belmont. There, he picked out the same kind of beeper that Fenwick wore for Madge.

Turner and Fenwick returned to Area Ten Headquarters. The building housing Area Ten was south of the River City complex on Wells Street on the southwest rim of Chicago's Loop. The building was as old and crumbling as River City was new and gleaming. Fifteen years ago, the department purchased a four-story warehouse scheduled for demolition and decreed it would be the new Area Ten Headquarters. Planned renovations occurred at random intervals. Lack of air-conditioning in the summer, was somewhat ameliorated by a huge numbers of fans nearly blowing their paperwork to uselessness. For the winter, all of the detectives, most of the clerks, and over half the uniformed cops, had brought in space heaters, making the entire complex a disaster waiting for a fire to destroy it.

Heavily bundled-up newspaper reporters huddled together just inside the doors to the station. As Turner and Fenwick walked in, the acting commander was giving a statement. Every time the doors opened, a swoosh of wind swirled in and lowered the temperature around the reporters ten degrees.

Turner and Fenwick hurried past the milling mob and up the stairs. At their desks on the third floor, they took out the beginnings of paperwork: Major Crime Worksheets, Daily Major Incident Logs, and Supplementary Reports.

Minutes later, the acting commander entered the room and strode over to them. The regular commander was on vacation in Cabo San Lucas. The acting commander was a Hispanic-American named Drew Molton, a sensible man who'd run afoul of the upper echelon of the Police Department. Last summer he'd had a one man show of his paintings in a local art gallery. While the money he made, from the sale of the pieces, had silenced most of the razzing from his cop buddies, neither the art, nor the amount of money earned kept the police brass from being leery about his artistic activities. A person achieving fame outside of the establishment made them uneasy.

Drew Molton sat down on the corner of Fenwick's desk. He said, "I hate it when famous people die. Makes the case a pain in the ass."

"I think I've got a problem with it," Turner said.

Molton gazed at him calmly and waited for him to explain.

It wasn't that Turner was unwilling to be open about his sexual orientation, he just wasn't eager to add another coming-out experience to his day's work. Unfortunately, coming out is a process, engaged in every time a new person or situation is met in which being openly gay is significant. It may be perfectly safe to come out, but each time it takes an emotional toll. Turner pulled in a lungful of air. "I'm gay and the dead guy was notoriously homophobic."

Molton looked at him in silence for several moments. Finally, he said, "And your point is?"

"I might not be able to be objective. What if some prosecutor tries to bring my feelings against him up at trial, like they did with that cop in Los Angeles?"

"That was negative feelings about the alleged killer, not the victim. It's not the same thing."

"In the same ballpark."

"I expect every cop in this command to respond to every situation professionally. If you want to tell me you can't handle it, then you're telling me you shouldn't be a detective. I'm sure that's not what you want to tell me. African-American cops investigate the murders of white bigots. White cops investigate the killings of angry African-Americans."

"This is an awfully high-profile case."

"That's why I'm glad you two are on it. I don't have to worry about screw-ups or prejudice. If you arrest somebody, it'll be done right, and I'll know we've got our killer. You two have the best conviction rate in the squad for the past three years." He pointed at Turner, "You ever make bigoted, antijudge, anti-straight comments?"

"No."

"Then you'll be a fine witness when we catch the asshole who did this."

Turner gazed at the Commander for a few moments. The vote of confidence made him feel good.

"I'm ordering you to stay on the case," the Commander finished. "Give me a full report after you're done today."

They nodded.

Molton added, "FBI might be nosing in on this one."

"Didn't happen anywhere they have jurisdiction," Fenwick said.

"Just the same, they'll probably be around. If the need arises, be as gentle with them as you can."

"Can we use anybody we want on the case?" Turner asked.

Milton said, "Within reason. Take Roosevelt and Wilson first. They're the best. A famous person is dead. I get pressure. You get pressure. We all get pressure. Let's get this over with as soon as we can." He left.

"Guess I'm on the case," Turner said.

They found Joe Roosevelt and Judy Wilson in the coffee room. Joe was red-nosed and short, with brush-cut gray hair and bad teeth. Judy was a fiercely competitive African-American woman. They had a well-deserved reputation as one of the most successful pairs of detectives on the force. When Turner and Fenwick entered the room, the other two detectives were arguing over what was appropriate to bring as a wedding gift when you were invited to a bachelor party or bridal shower but not to the wedding or reception itself.

Roosevelt turned on them, "You guys decide . . ."

Wilson interrupted, "I'm not asking two males what is socially appropriate. How are they going to know?"

"Why would I care?" Fenwick asked.

Turner had heard Roosevelt and Wilson raising their voices to each other on everything from the most appropriate caliber of gun a cop should keep in reserve to the politics in the Streets and Sanitation Department in the city. He figured they must take delight in disagreeing since, over the years, neither had ever requested a transfer. Turner forestalled resumption in this latest round of debates, diverting their attention to the case at hand.

"We need you to take charge of the canvass of the neighborhood on the Judge Meade case."

"Figured you'd need our help," Roosevelt said. "What's the story?"

"Somebody popped him in the middle of the forehead," Fenwick said. "Left him to freeze in an alley near Lincoln and Fullerton."

"Judgesicle," Wilson said.

"We've got McWilliams and a couple others out in the field freezing their butts off," Fenwick said.

"But you'd rather it be us," Wilson said.

"Copsicles," Roosevelt said.

"Yeah, but you won't be dead," Fenwick said.

"Right," Wilson said. "We only had thirty other cases we were working on."

"Doesn't everybody?" Turner said.

"Who's got the results on the pool?" Roosevelt asked.

"I'm not sure," Fenwick said. "Couple people passed it around. I put my time on the sheet and gave my money to one of the uniforms downstairs."

"I'm working on a three-thirty dead bum," Wilson said. "I think I've got a chance."

Turner and Fenwick returned to their desks in the squad room.

Randy Carruthers entered and hurried over toward them. Fenwick groaned. "There's gotta be a law against stupidity and the penalty has got to be having your head chopped off."

"Carruthers wouldn't miss his."

"Yeah, what little brains he's got are in his butt."

"Hi, you guys." Randy wore a green, knit turtleneck sweater. The collar was caught in the folds of his double chin. The bulges of fat on his torso protruded prominently under the tight-fitting garment. He plopped his substantial butt on the corner of Fenwick's desk. Commanders and acting commanders could safely intrude on Fenwick's space. Anyone lower in rank perched at their own peril. No matter how many times Fenwick's ham hand had swiped at Carruthers' ass, the rotund nuisance never got the message.

Fenwick's paw moved quickly. Carruthers jumped.

"Where's Rodriguez?" Fenwick asked. Rodriguez was Carruthers' long-suffering partner. Six years ago, Rodriguez had offended the wrong member of the police power structure and he was certain they'd assigned him to Carruthers in revenge.

"Haven't seen him in half an hour. He said we were supposed to go check out a report of someone carrying coal to Newcastle. I've never heard of that part of the city. He said I'm supposed to look it up and find it. I didn't know people still heated their homes with coal. Course, it's so cold, you never can tell."

"Good luck," Fenwick said. He made a show of returning to his work. Turner was already filling in the tops of several forms.

"But I got to tell you guys," Carruthers said. "That Judge Meade, you've got to find who killed him. He was the finest man who ever sat on the federal bench."

"Didn't know you knew him," Turner said.

"I didn't, but I followed his cases for years. He was showing those liberals a thing or two. He knew how to deal with them. I went to a talk he gave once."

Turner looked up and gave him an interested look. Actually being listened to brought a grin to Carruthers' face. Turner could see the off-yellow front tooth mixed with the other grayish ones.

"When was this?" Turner asked.

"When I was taking classes at DePaul." Carruthers was eternally taking classes. He'd tried law school but never went beyond a semester. He'd never got into the Social Worker program he'd applied to. "He came to make a speech. About fifty people attended."

"What'd he say?" Turner asked.

"Just talked about returning America to family values. He spoke like someone who knew what he was talking about. Quoted statistics. He was very inspirational."

"Nothing radical? Any angry questions from the crowd?"

"No. At the end we stood up and cheered. It felt odd in a room with only fifty people, but I didn't care. I liked what he said."

Fenwick gave a rumble deep in his throat. Carruthers stepped back several paces. Fenwick said, "Randy, I think I hear your mother calling. Good-bye."

They returned to their paperwork.

Carruthers gave them both confused looks which neither of them saw. He stared at the tops of their heads a moment and then left.

Half an hour later, Turner's phone rang. It was Ian.

"Rumor has it you've got a dead Nazi on your hands," Ian said.

"How do you know these things?"

"Sources. Are you working on the Meade case?"

"Yes," Paul said.

"He was a hateful twit."

"I already know Judge Meade was not a member of the bench esteemed in the gay community."

"I'm organizing the celebration among all my friends."

"How many gay people really would have known who he was?"

"Me. A few attorneys. I only know because I've written articles after this circuit has ruled on cases of interest to us. I attended lectures he gave."

"Carruthers says he's been to a lecture the judge gave. Are you guys secretly best friends?"

Ian snorted. "That man is certifiably straight, and I for one am glad of it. I didn't see Carruthers at any lecture I was at."

Turner asked, "Aren't judges supposed to be impartial? If they speak out, aren't they prejudicing their cases or prejudging, or something?"

"Lots of them give talks and state their opinions. They feel they are founts of wisdom. They get chauffeured to work. They are nasty, egotistical, and self-important. They have no idea what is going on in the real world."

"That sounds a little harsh."

"As far as I'm concerned they should have killed more than one."

"I'll keep that in mind if federal judges all across the country suddenly start flopping over dead. Who else would recognize his name?" Turner asked.

"All the people who read my byline in the paper and my columns, if both of them are in town that week. Not that many, unfortunately."

"Going to be a sort of a small celebration."

"We will make up in quality what we lack in quantity. Want to come?"

"No. I'm sure I'll be busy until late. I do memorize all your columns and I don't remember his name coming up."

"Perhaps you've been fibbing to me all this time."

"I treasure every syllable you write. Maybe I was on vacation when his name came up."

"They're leaving you on the case?"

"Yes."

"Good for them. He was an evil man. You find out who did it, he or she could become a big hero."

"Still just a dead body with a killer to catch. Why did you call, Ian?"

"To get the low-down inside dirt and cheap, tawdry gossip about the case."

"And pigs can fly."

"I think I saw that in a bar I was in the other night. Or maybe I was hallucinating."

"Hallucinating," Turner confirmed.

"You haven't been in some of the bars I've been in lately. Actually I have a tip that we can't possibly print. At least not for a while. My source on this is very unreliable. Maybe I'll learn more as the day goes on. I've got the rather startling rumor that the dead judge was in a gay bar on the north side last night."

"Which bar?"

"He wouldn't say."

"That sure narrows it down. How much credence do you except me to give to this?"

"Enough so that, if it turns out to be true and I'm the source, I get an exclusive if you guys find somebody to arrest?"

"Do I get to talk to the source?"

"Maybe."

"In that case, that's my answer. You say the source is unreliable."

"Highly."

"Get back to me when you get to trustworthy. I'm not going to believe some late-night, twinkie pick-up of yours."

"I am offended. It was not late and not last night." Ian sighed. "I'll try to convince him to let you interview him. I'm also going to keep working on my other sources in the gay community which, as you know, are legion. I smell a big story in this. I'm going to bust my butt on it."

"Call me if you get something useful."

Turner and Fenwick organized details and assignments for

another half-an-hour. They made phone calls and connections before setting out to conduct their next interviews. The most basic was to the airline to check if someone had used the judge's ticket. The official from the airline confirmed that the ticket had been purchased some months ago and paid for with a credit card but had not been used last night. No one had tried to get a refund. He was sorry to hear of the judge's death and promised to cancel the debt.

Turner hung up and gave this information to Fenwick. "So he was planning to go," Turner finished.

"Or it was a clever dodge."

"Or something prevented him from leaving."

"There's a bunch we don't know yet."

Minutes later, they left, taking a photo of the judge with them to show. The bitter wind howled as they drove away from the station. The weather forecast called for possible record cold overnight.

They stopped at Aunt Millie's Bar and Grill for a brief, late lunch. They found Rodriguez hunched in what had become, over the years, the booth in the back that Area Ten detectives called their own. Aunt Millie's was one of the last vestiges of a grittier Chicago past in the recently upscale Printers Row area of the city on Dearborn Street just south of Congress Parkway. There had been rumors early last fall that it was going to be closed down by the city but, the day after the local cops heard about it, the rumors died abruptly. Cops packed the place at mealtimes and before and after each shift change, though, no matter what time of day or night, or even what item was ordered, all the food on the menu seemed to come out as mounds of artery-clogging glop.

A waitress in a pink poodle skirt and rhinestone-studded glasses took their order.

Rodriguez said, "Tell me good news. He died and I'm free."

"Who?" Fenwick asked.

"The blob from hell."

"Last I saw Carruthers he was looking up coals in the encyclopedia."

"Dumb shit."

"He's been worse than usual lately," Fenwick said.

"I hate how sunny and cheerful he is around the holidays," Rodriguez said. "I thought him being gone that week before Christmas would be a relief, but he just got more frenzied before he left. Think about it. Who tried to organize that gift exchange? Who wanted everybody to get together for a drink on Christmas Eve? Who wanted everybody's family to get together? Who wanted to play Santa Claus to all the little kids in the neighborhood?"

"That last one was me," Fenwick said. "I've got the build for it, and I like little kids. I've done it off and on for years."

"Not my fault," Rodriguez said. "Anyway, he tried to do the rest of them and more. Being with him at the holidays makes me want to start a Scrooge Fan Club. I bet lots of people would join. 'Bah, humbug' is a highly underrated response to the holiday season."

Their food arrived.

"Heard you got a dead judge."

"Judgesicle," Fenwick said.

Rodriguez grinned. "I like that. What time did he come in at?"

"Seven forty-five."

"I've still got a chance on the pool then. I had six thirty-six. I may be closest."

"There's got to be somebody earlier," Fenwick said. "I can't be out of the pool. It's at least five hundred bucks. What's wrong with the criminal element in Chicago? How can they let a little cold stop them? It's New Year's for Christ's sake. You'd think a little murder and mayhem would be a great way to start the year."

"You'll have to talk to Dwayne and Ashley. Last I knew, they had the sheet."

Dwayne Smythe and Ashley Devonshire were the newest additions to the detective squad at Area Ten. Everybody hated their know-it-all attitude and their inability to make arrests stick. They'd lost three major cases in the last month. The fresh-faced rookies had avoided Aunt Millie's since they lost the last one.

"Heard the dead judge was a homophobic creep," Rodriguez said.

"That's out on the street already?"

"On the radio. Your buddy Ian Hume was quoted on several of the all-news stations."

"I didn't know the judge's name until today," Turner said. "How many of us know the names of federal judges, and we're cops? We don't get a lot of cases that go to them. I bet ninety-nine percent of the people in this city couldn't name a federal judge, beyond one or two from the Supreme Court."

"And that's bad?"

"That's typical."

They finished their meal and left. The first person they were to interview was the chief judge of the Seventh Federal Judicial Circuit, James S. Wadsworth.

6

Judge Wadsworth lived on Lake Shore Drive in a luxury high-rise apartment just north of Erie Street. He'd offered to meet them, however, in his chambers in the new Kennedy Federal Building, just north of Congress Parkway at the south end of the Loop and only a few blocks from Aunt Millie's. He could gain them entrance to inspect Judge Meade's office.

The red steel and glass structure was across from the new Cook County Jail. The brand-new Kennedy Federal Building was something of a joke among Chicagoans. Every once in a while, a public building went up and was plagued with glitches. The State of Illinois Building had huge problems with heating and air-conditioning, among numerous others. From rats in the offices to leaks in the roof, the less-than-two-year-old Kennedy Building had come in for lots of criticism. One of the funnier headlines had been on the need to replace all the doorknobs in the building. Someone had ordered them all a half-size too small. The rumor was that the architect was living luxuriously in Tahiti.

The judge met them at the security desk and they took the elevator to the tenth floor. The judge's chamber was all blond wood, maroon leather, and bookcases crammed with books. He had a window that looked east over the Harold Washington Library to Lake Michigan, south on Dearborn, and even a little west to the Midwest Stock Exchange Building, which bridged the Parkway.

The judge was a tall, slender, handsome man in his early sixties, wearing blue jeans and a white fisherman's sweater. He greeted them gravely.

After they were seated he said, "This is a tragedy. We haven't had a federal judge murdered in years. I don't know if we ever have. This is awful. He was a good judge."

"Was he?" Fenwick asked.

Wadsworth's responding look was not hostile. He said, "I think carefully about all the people who work in this jurisdiction. I make it a practice never to criticize my fellow jurists. Certainly not after they're dead."

"Meaning there was something to criticize about Meade?" Fenwick asked.

"That is certainly not what I meant," Wadsworth said. "I speak very precisely. My words mean exactly what they say. None of us is perfect. Have you not made poor decisions or committed blunders you later regretted?"

"We didn't get murdered last night," Fenwick said.

Turner noted that Judge Wadsworth paused before each sentence. His face, clear and unlined in repose, crinkled from mouth to chin whether frowning or trying to smile. The crinkling occurred before the beginning of each statement. A message of superiority, wisdom, thoughtfulness, and great weight was given to his every utterance.

"We need to know the dynamics of the court here," Turner said. "Somebody was angry enough to kill him."

"Not anybody here. This was a group of men and women who took their jobs seriously. These were people who knew they were given grave responsibilities and who worked hard to fulfill them. I'm sure none of them is guilty of any transgression."

"Didn't his rabid conservatism antagonize his fellow jurists?" Fenwick asked.

"No. You can look through all his decisions. Examine the

record. You'll see that he was with the majority more often than not. He was not isolated or alone. He had friends here."

"What about the public attacks on him?"

"There is often controversy following our rulings. When you are in our position you have to expect that. Attacks are part of the job. Certainly no one presumes there will be physical danger. Nobody made an attempt on the life of a Supreme Court Judge over *Roe* v. *Wade* or the subsequent decisions connected to that case."

"But people have died because of that issue."

"Not judges."

Wadsworth was not aware of any personal animosities among the jurists, clerks, and any other employee. Nor did he know of any family troubles Meade might have had. In answer to their question, Wadsworth claimed he was at a political fund-raiser most of the afternoon then drove home with his wife and, subsequently, spent a quiet evening with her.

They got the names and addresses of the people who worked closely with Judge Meade. If they had time, they'd get to them today at home. If not, most would be in to work tomorrow.

Wadsworth called one of the security guards and, with him, accompanied them to Meade's office. With bringing Mrs. Meade down to make positive identification, they hadn't had time to inspect any papers at Meade's home to see if they were significant or not.

The security guard opened the door.

Judge Wadsworth stood in the entrance. He said, "I'll leave you. The security guard will be outside the door, in case you need anything."

And to watch so they didn't steal the silver, Turner thought.

Fenwick's first comment, after the door shut behind them, was, "Knowing my public servants are so perfect and dedicated sure cheers me up. I'm comforted that they got along so well."

"Can't have been that much sweetness and light. There had

to be disagreements. We'll have to check all these people as well as Meade's recent cases. We better see if we can get some researchers started reading those things."

The room had more maroon leather, blond wood, and bookcases crammed with books. The only difference between this room and Judge Wadsworth's was it had a south and west corner view. From this office you could see the top half of the Sears Tower.

Fenwick took down a few of the books at leisure. "All the judges offices I've ever been in or seen on television have these rows of books. I wonder if they ever really open them."

Turner shrugged.

One door led off to a darkened courtroom. Behind another was a pristine clean bathroom, complete with shower and fresh towels.

"This so he could clean up after a hard day of judging?" Fenwick asked.

"I guess."

Turner opened the medicine cabinet. They gazed inside.

Fenwick said, "Just once I'd like to open one of these and have it make a difference in a case." Nothing in the bathroom was remotely suspicious.

They sifted carefully through the documents strewn on top of the judge's desk.

After several minutes of skimming through one document Fenwick began to sing, "Clues, glorious clues."

"Find something?"

"No. Just aimlessly humming."

"You were singing. You were using words. Singing—words. Humming—no words. I'm beginning to worry about you, Buck. You've been singing Broadway show tunes a lot lately."

"And learning the basics of color and fabric. I think it's just a phase."

"You see an appointment book?"

Fenwick shook his head.

Turner glanced at the family picture on the desk. In it the

judge still had all his hair. The family was in a woods or a very large backyard having a picnic. They all sat around a table with a red-checked tablecloth. Besides the judge and his wife, there was a girl about eight or nine and a boy about four or five.

They started through the drawers. After twenty minutes of paper clips, pens, papers, and a paperback novel of Barbara D'Amato's *Hard Christmas,* they had nothing helpful in the murder investigation.

Fenwick slammed the bottom drawer shut and said, "I got plenty of nothing."

"Stop that," Turner said, "or I'll tell Carruthers."

They left.

Judge Rosemary Malmsted, assistant chief judge, was next on their list. She lived in the western suburb of Oak Brook and had not been willing to drive into the city. Using their map, they quickly arrived at her substantial trilevel home on Apple Street.

They heard a football game on in a distant living room as she led them into a sitting room. In one corner sat a chest of drawers decoupaged with scenes of Paris. A leather sofa and matching love seats with chrome accents were placed around a glass-top coffee table. This last rested on top of a Chinese Deco carpet.

Judge Malmsted wore baggy, black jeans, a flannel sweater, and black leather boots.

Turner said, "We talked to Judge Wadsworth about Judge Meade and we'll be talking to all your colleagues."

"Our esteemed leader told you everything was wonderful, didn't he? That everyone worked together like a family?"

"Not precisely. He did say you all got along."

She gave a low, mirthless laugh. "He's wrong."

"What can you tell us?" Fenwick asked.

"I can tell you my perceptions. I don't think there was enough wrong to drive someone to murder, but my information might give you places to go, people to talk to, and angles to think about—which is the point of an investigation, isn't it?"

Turner and Fenwick nodded.

"I've been on the bench here for two years. I was appointed by a Democrat. Meade was one of Nixon's last appointees. Made it to the bench as a young man. I believe his family made fairly substantial contributions to Republican coffers, as did mine to Democrats, before I was elevated to the bench. Judges don't like to talk about such things, but it is the truth."

A cheer erupted from the distant television. She poked her head out the door. "Turn that down, Arnie," she called, then returned to her seat.

"You will discover, from those of us on the bench in Chicago who are honest, that I hated him."

Turner and Fenwick simply kept giving her their best, "the witness is talking and I'm going to listen" faces.

"You don't act surprised."

"Should we be?" Turner asked.

She shrugged. "I don't think any of the others had as much animosity between them as he and I. At least they never expressed it as much as the two of us did. I am considered the most liberal of the judges. Meade was the most conservative. In our meetings, we were always on the opposite side. It would have been different if he was arguing from logical and sensible theories, philosophies, or beliefs. He was just a hater. A blind bigot."

"The hatred was mutual?"

"Oh, yes. Everybody saw it at least once."

"Judge Wadsworth?"

"Of course he did. The old hypocrite. He's big on decorum, secrets, and the 'old boy' network. I wish he'd retire or die. Either one works for me."

"That work for you in terms of Judge Meade?"

She smiled. "I was speaking rhetorically, not making a statement of intent or describing an action taken."

"Where were you last night?" Fenwick asked.

"Here. We had a family gathering that lasted until two in the morning. My mother and father are in town, vacationing for the holidays. We were up around seven this morning."

"Tell me about his conservative decisions," Turner said.

"Think of all the issues of the day. Abortion, gay rights, affirmative action, drug testing, redistricting. If he had his way, every woman would be pregnant, tested for drugs, not allowed to vote, and married to a man who was the only one in the house out earning an income."

"He antagonized a lot of groups?" Fenwick asked.

"Well, he wasn't as prominent a conservative as, say, a Phyllis Schlafly or a Pat Buchanan, but in his own way he had more impact than they ever did. Our decisions often have an immediate, direct effect on those involved."

"Any ones in particular come to mind?"

"Of course, the latest was the upholding of the antigay law in Du Page County."

"Before that?"

"I'd have to check dates and decisions. He's been around a long time. He's got a paper trail you'll have to follow, although he didn't write a lot of the decisions."

"Who did?"

"He was a hater, but he wasn't too bright. Whoever was on the bench and could be articulate about his position would write the decision."

"Did he prevail often?"

"We've been getting a little more liberal. Sometimes he won, sometimes he lost. I'd say in the past few years he'd lost more than won, mostly because he was so stupid. People were getting fed up with him just being negative and inarticulate."

"Other than disagree with you, could he actually cause you problems."

"Like what?"

"Try and lose you your job?"

"Meade would threaten and bluster, but that kind of thing doesn't really happen. There is a judicial review that the chief judge runs, but it is very secret and very unknown. We do have a good-behavior clause but, in essence, we serve for life. All the judges could get together and recommend someone be fired, but I've never heard of it happening. More likely, people would talk to a judge and try and get him or her to step down."

"He threatened to get your job?"

"Judge Meade could make intemperate comments. I'd learned not to take them seriously."

In the car Turner said, "Thank you Richard Nixon."

Their car radio crackled with their name on it. "I got a message for Turner. Says here to meet a guy named Hume. He's at someplace called the *Gay Tribune,* and he says it's important."

"He must have our witness," Turner said.

"We need to look into these judges," Fenwick said. "A hotbed of dissent right in front of us."

"My this-is-our-killer-radar hasn't gone off yet."

"When did you get yours installed?"

"Carruthers had one and I was jealous."

7

They drove back to the city, looping through the mistake in the suburbs where traffic from three major highways converged into just three lanes of the Eisenhower Expressway. Even with the light holiday traffic, there was a delay. In the city, they took the Ashland Avenue exit off the Eisenhower north to Belmont and then east to Broadway. The offices of the paper were on the east side of Broadway where Buckingham dead-ended. The three-story building was built in the last year by the owner of the paper, who discovered the *Gay Tribune* had turned into small gold mine. The owner rented out a third of the top floor to a gay law firm. During the Pride Parade last June, they draped what they claimed was the largest rainbow flag in Chicago from the roof.

They parked in the bus stop at Melrose and Broadway. The walk to the paper chilled them thoroughly.

A secretary directed them up two flights of stairs to Ian's office. Computers were strewn amid the modern polished chrome-accent pieces, all softened by the deep gold carpeting, recessed track lighting, and pleasantly overstuffed chairs grouped around solid oak coffee tables. Even on the holiday, several people were hunched over computers. Thursday was deadline day.

Ian met them at the top of the stairs and led them to an office that was the opposite of the pristine neatness outside. Before he opened the door, he said, "This is not the guy who talked to me first. I found someone more reliable."

"How?" Turner asked.

"Sources," Ian answered.

Turner frowned. He hoped they didn't get into a fight about who was getting information from whom and what needed to be revealed.

They entered Ian's office. Tattered posters of long-closed art exhibitions covered two of the walls. Huge maps of the city covered another wall. One map had congressional districts drawn on it, another had the state legislative districts outlined, and there was a third with all the wards in the city indicated. Corkboard covered the wall around the door. Messages crammed all the space around all three sides of the opening. On the edges of the chaos were several beefcake calendars, not all of them from the New Year. All but one were turned to months with pictures of extremely attractive men. The newest one had Mr. January in western gear. Turner liked the one from June of 1987. That picture showed a slender, bare-chested man in tight black, leather pants, straddling a sleek, black motorcycle.

When they entered the room, a lanky young man stood up. Ian introduced him as Billy Geary.

Ian sat in the nicked-and-scarred wooden swivel chair. With his right index finger he shoved his slouch fedora far back on his head. Billy perched on the edge of the desk. He wore black warm-up pants, a white hooded sweatshirt that said Oxford, and black running shoes. The bulky clothes did not hide the fact that he had broad shoulders and a narrow waist. Fenwick leaned against a file cabinet on the far side of the room. Turner rested against a blank space on the corkboard wall. The four of them filled the small room and made the atmosphere seem close.

"You guys are cops?" Geary asked.

They showed their identification.

Geary nodded. "I wasn't sure about this. I'm still not definite, but once I heard that Judge Meade was dead, I figured I'd better tell somebody. Then Ian called."

"I've been tracking down everybody I know who had any connection with the courts. I met Billy at . . ." Ian hesitated.

Geary said, "I'm not doing anything illegal, and I'm not ashamed of what I do. I'm a dancer at Au Naturel, and I go to law school at Loyola."

"How does that work?" Fenwick asked.

Geary looked confused. "I don't understand what you mean."

"They don't seem like compatible professions," Fenwick said.

"Why not? I don't dance on the tables at the school. I don't bring my books to study at the bar."

"Just curious," Fenwick said. "But why do you do it?"

"I need a job to get myself through school. My parents threw me out of the house when I told them I was gay. The money is good. I make more than anybody I know on their side job. It's better than toting barges and lifting bales and I like the attention. It also helps that I'm an exhibitionist."

"What's your connection with Judge Meade?" Turner asked.

"I had a project last spring in one of my classes. It was on federal appellate decisions. They've got that terrific library in the new Kennedy Federal Building so I was down there a lot. I stopped in a few of the courtrooms and I wound up listening to the arguments in the Du Page County case. You know the one about the gay rights?"

"We know," Fenwick said.

Geary looked surprised.

Turner said, "So you knew Judge Meade by sight?"

"Yes. The important thing is, I saw him last night."

"Where?"

"In Au Naturel."

"You're sure?" Turner asked.

"It was only a quick glimpse. Some guy had just dropped a

ten dollar bill in my G-string. That's ten times what we're used to so I'd given him a little more than a hug and a peck for his efforts. He offered me . . ." Geary looked at Ian.

Ian said, "You can tell them about the offer. Don't go beyond that."

"You his lawyer?" Fenwick asked.

"Go ahead, Billy," Ian said.

Geary nodded. "I was startled at the amount of money he offered me to go home with him later that night."

Ian said, "The dancers are often offered gifts and favors."

"And money," Turner said. "Let's get on with it. We're not here to bust you for prostitution."

Geary said, "This was about eleven. I wasn't sure where I was going after work, and he offered me more than the going rate. I told the guy I'd have to let him know. He was nice about it. I gave him an extra nuzzle or two and he, well, never mind about that."

Grabbing the crotch of, pulling the G-string out and catching a peek at, and rubbing the front of the dancers were not uncommon practices. Turner always figured the owners must pay a high amount of graft to keep from being hassled by vice.

"I got done with that guy. I was standing up, and right behind him was Judge Meade."

"What was he doing?"

"He wasn't looking at me. He was trying to get past the dance floor area. It was really crowded so it took him a while. I doubt if he would recognize me. He couldn't possibly know me. There was always a crowd in his courtroom, besides I was wearing a lot less last night than when I was in his courtroom."

"Did he give you money?"

"No. I don't know where he went, how long he stayed, or what he did. I only saw him that once. He disappeared, and I kept dancing. I didn't see him the rest of the night."

"When did you find out he died?"

"After Ian called. I didn't get up until after one today. I ate breakfast and watched some football games. I turned on the local news during halftime."

"Billy was my nineteenth call. I was deep into my list of sources. Luck."

Turner asked Billy, "You sure it was him?"

"I'd testify to it in court."

"Did you mention it to anybody else last night?"

"When I got back to our dressing room, I made a general announcement. I couldn't believe that a notorious homophobe was in Au Naturel. I assumed it meant that he was a closet case. Typical, one of our own persecuting us the most. Thank you J. Edgar Hoover."

"What did the other dancers say?"

"Not much. Most of them aren't very political. We're all pretty young. The guys are out for a good time and to make money. I had to explain to a couple of them who he was and that he was antigay."

"Tell me about the dancers," Fenwick said. "I need some sense of who they are or who they hope to become."

"They're just guys. Some are straight. Majority are gay."

"I mean, what do they do when they aren't dancing? They all aren't in law school or visiting courtrooms?"

"I don't know a lot of them. A few are in school like me. Most of us do a little hustling on the side. Lots of them live in cheap apartments. They spend all their money on partying, alcohol, and drugs, especially drugs. A lot of them sleep until three in the afternoon. After you get up, if you've got half a brain, you go to a gym and work out or at least jog or run—do something to keep in shape. Then you dance and party and go nuts. It can be lots of fun."

"How do they get out of the business?"

"Some become full-time hustlers. Most just drift into other things. A few try to be those dancers for hire at parties. It's a life that doesn't have a lot of benefits or a pension program. A rare few find, and are able to settle down with, a sugar daddy.

Doesn't happen often. I've heard of it but I don't know anyone that has actually happened to."

"At Au Naturel do the guys run into problems with customers being too forward or too friendly?"

"A few clients get a little rambunctious. Mostly not."

"The pay is worth it?"

"Sure. I like money. As for Judge Meade, if he was a closet case, the dancers would have loved him."

"Why?"

"One of the guys said it for all of us, 'those closet cases may be a pain, but they pay the most money.' Which is true. Closeted guys tend to pay a lot."

"Blackmail?" Fenwick asked.

Geary laughed. "A prostitute has some honor. Do whores and their clients really even know each other's real names or care much even if they do? Unless they're long-term clients or long-term whores? In which case, the relationship is different. Why bust up a steady meal ticket?"

Turner stuffed the blackmail possibility high on his questions-to-ask list.

"If it isn't blackmail, why do they pay more?" Fenwick asked.

"Stupidity? Desperation? Gratitude? Maybe it's a sort of blackmail pay-off in their own minds, or a making up for guilt, a way of salving their consciences? You'd have to ask them or someone who's a prostitute. At Au Naturel, you pay a dollar for at most a few seconds of touching. If you figure out why men go to prostitutes, you could write a book and be famous."

"Somebody probably already has," Fenwick said. "Anybody mention to you if they saw him the rest of the night?"

"No, but I didn't ask either. I don't know any more than I've already told you. It was such a crazy night, and he's not the first politician to be in there." He paused, then said, "This is big-time news, isn't it?"

Turner nodded. "We'd prefer it if you didn't talk to the press."

Fenwick said, "We could become a lot less understanding of your recreational activities if this becomes a front-page headline."

"Ian's a reporter and he knows."

Everybody looked at Ian.

Ian said, "We'll have to see. Leave Billy out of it. You can deal with me on that."

They took down Billy's address and phone number. After he left Ian said, "What a tangled web we weave."

"Why are we quoting Shakespeare?" Fenwick asked.

Ian said to Turner, "You owe me ten bucks."

"Why?"

"Last night—I didn't pay the guy."

"I don't see any proof." Turner explained the bet from the night before to Fenwick. Then he said, "Ben and I were in Au Naturel last night. So was Ian."

"So were half the gay people in the city," Ian said.

"But most of that half is not investigating this case."

"Did either of you see the judge?" Fenwick asked.

"I didn't," Turner said. "I wouldn't have recognized him if I did." He pulled the photo of the judge out of his regulation-blue notebook and gazed at it. He shook his head. "The face doesn't ring a bell. I was more concerned with Ben."

"You bring a date to a dancing bar?" Fenwick asked.

"You mean a bar with dancing men or women?" Ian corrected."

"Either."

"Why not?" Ian asked.

"I wouldn't bring Madge to a place like that. I can picture her hooting as the men put money in some floozy's crotch."

"You wouldn't take her because she'd laugh, carry on, and make fun," Turner said.

"She'd have too damn good of a time," Fenwick said.

"It was a place to go and have fun," Ian said.

Turner added, "Although it is none of your business, neither

Ben nor I put money in any part of anybody's clothing last night."

"I think they're both too shy," Ian said. "I've been trying to get them over their hang-ups."

"Is my being there going to compromise the case?"

"Don't see why it should," Fenwick said, "You didn't see anything. It was a coincidence, pure and simple."

"I don't believe in coincidences and neither do you, Buck." Turner sighed. "I am more concerned about Ben. I don't want him involved in an investigation."

"I think this blackmail angle has real possibilities," Fenwick said. "I don't care what Billy said about the nobility of whores not blackmailing their clients."

"I can see the headlines," Turner said, "notorious homophobe in love nest with male prostitute. We'll have to keep it in mind."

"You guys remember Geary from last night?" Fenwick asked.

Turner shook his head. Ian nodded.

"So, now what?" Ian asked.

"I thank you for the big tip. We find out the name of the owner of the bar. Interview him or her . . ."

Ian said, "Owner is Dana Sickles. Has a solid reputation in the community. Supports a lot of good causes. I can try and dig up some information on her for you."

"Thanks. We'll see her and all the employees of the bar, including the dancers."

Ian said, "You want to stay on the case because secretly you're a lech. This way you get to talk to all the guys up close and personal."

Turner ignored him and continued, "Then see if anybody else saw him. Don't figure on a lot of people coming forward to volunteer that they were there last night."

It was an odd thing about the gay community. Many of the people who were at the bar last night would say they were openly gay, at least to varying degrees. However, there would be enormous hesitation about coming forward and admitting they were present—especially if something criminal was known to be involved. This was a historical problem in the gay community everywhere, although there had been specific local difficulties over time. Not more than a year ago in Chicago, there had been a negative incident. Every patron of a gay bar, more than fifty, had been ordered by the police to lie on the floor. They were then searched. The police claimed they had evidence that one of the patrons possessed drugs. The ACLU was interested in helping with the case, thinking that the suspected patron could have been searched but not every person in the bar, and that the constitutional rights of all the others had been violated. The difficulty had been in getting any of those who'd been present to come forward and testify. Other than the employees of the bar, only a few brave souls had been willing to speak out. Fear and mistrust of the police among gay people went back much further than just to the Stonewall Inn in New York back in 1969.

Turner and Fenwick left the newspaper offices.

In the car Turner said, "Well, that about tears it. How many cops do you know who were at a possible crime scene before it happened? It would add me to the suspect list. If I pursue the case, it's like I'm trying to let myself off the hook."

"We don't know it's the crime scene. Did you kill him?"

"Thanks for asking. No."

"Did Ben?"

"No."

"Did Ian?"

"He's a little radical, but not nuts. He takes out his anger in the editorials and columns he writes."

"So nobody you know did the killing. What's the problem? Having you on the case might give us important information. In fact it already has."

"Gay people, cops, or both could accuse me of selling out."

"Or you could just do your job and stop whining."

"I am not whining."

"You're coming closer than any time since I've known you."

"If I ever whine, just pull out your gun and shoot me."

"I can live with that."

"Figured." Turner looked at his watch. "It's after five. Why don't we stop at the bar? We might catch the owner there, or we can find out where she lives. We can start the questioning. At least we've got a notion on where Meade was last night."

"And blackmail as a possible motive."

"Does this clear up the paid-for plane ticket problem?" Turner asked.

"I dunno," Fenwick said.

"If he was a closet case, the whole trip could have been an elaborate deception designed to fool the wife and kiddies."

"People are that desperate to hide?"

"Lots are. He might have been. If somebody ever outed him after all the grief he's caused gay people, it could be a major scandal. At the least, his marriage would be in deep trouble, most probably over. Just realizing he was gay could have been enough stress to put him over the edge."

"You went through a hell of a lot of stress, but you handled it."

"Took a long time, and I was no saint."

Turner's wife had died when Jeff was born. In the months before his second's son's birth, Paul had come to accept being gay. He'd come to love his wife as a friend and her death had pained him deeply. He sometimes wondered what would have happened had she lived and had he come out to her. Certainly their marriage would have been over. It was one of the great "what ifs" of his life.

"I want to check in with Roosevelt and Wilson before we do more questioning," Turner said.

"Murder victims need to get organized," Fenwick said. "A little timetable of their movements would be helpful, or a few more witnesses to the dastardly deeds."

"You're hallucinating again, Buck."

Fenwick banged his fist on the dashboard. "Ah, reality. I feel so much better."

They called the station. Roosevelt and Wilson's last known location was on Lincoln Avenue near the coffee shop at the end of Montana Street.

8

In the coffee shop, the large picture windows were covered with steam. Patches of ice clung to the corners of the interior of the windows. They found Detectives Roosevelt and Wilson talking to two uniformed cops. Turner and Fenwick pulled over two chairs to sit with them. They were the only patrons. De Paul University, only a block or two away, wasn't in session, so even brave or demented college students wouldn't be out on a night like this. The locals knew better. Not even a crazed jogger, numerous ones of whom infested this neighborhood, disturbed the deserted sidewalks outside.

"What have you got?" Turner asked.

"Nothing from any of the residents," an older cop in the best big-gut florid-face tradition of the Chicago Police Department said. "We stopped in as many of the businesses as we could. Not many were open. There's a gay bar called Au Naturel where we tried to talk to people. There was a little bit of a crowd, but we got no help. Nobody would talk to us. The owner was a little snotty. She called her lawyer while we were there."

"Sounds suspicious," Wilson said.

"Or a canny gay bar owner being careful," Turner said.

"We'll check it out," Fenwick said. "Anything else?"

The uniformed cops shook their heads. They left.

Turner and Fenwick explained their tip about the judge being in Au Naturel.

"This Geary guy was sure it was Judge Meade?"

"Claimed to be," Fenwick said.

Roosevelt shook his head. "We've got lots of call backs to make. We're also checking into the possibility of a cab driver having dropped him off, especially if the judge drove all the way in from the airport to here. They'd remember that."

"Wife said he liked to use the El," Turner said.

"A federal judge?" Roosevelt asked, "In this cold?"

"The rich get more plebeian," Wilson said.

"Where's his luggage?" Fenwick asked. "I just thought of that." He explained what they'd learned from Mrs. Meade.

"He have a ticket or key to one of those luggage lockers at the airport when you went through his pockets?" Wilson asked.

"Not that we found," Fenwick said.

"I don't think they have those anymore," Turner said. "I think it was an antiterrorist thing years ago. Mad bombers kept putting bombs in them. You get rid of the lockers, the insane have one less venue to vent their spleen in. I haven't seen them in any train stations, and I don't remember them at the airport when I took Brian out there."

"So where's his luggage? Must have taken it out to the airport. Mrs. Meade would have wondered where it was when he left."

"In his office?"

"No, we already looked through it."

"Maybe the luggage went to Canada but he didn't?"

"We'll have to find out," Fenwick said. "Where do we go next?"

"The testy bar owner," Turner said. "Let's find out what the story is there. If her lawyer is still around, it might help."

They drove to Au Naturel. Fenwick parked in the bus stop out front and they walked in.

About ten people slumped on chairs around the front bar. A few watched a football game on a large screen television. Several glanced occasionally at a dancer who had to be at least in his late fifties. The guy was in great shape, but no question he was soon going to be eligible for social security. No one approached him with money to stuff into his bright red thong. Turner saw the dancer yawn. Late night last night for everybody.

They approached the bar and asked to speak to the owner.

"Now what?" The bartender said. He was in his midtwenties. He wore faded blue jeans, a flannel shirt with the sleeves cut off, and a leather vest.

They took out their identification and showed him. He picked up the phone and punched two numbers. He turned his head away and spoke into the receiver.

Turner noted two men get up and sidle past them and out the door. Cop identification in a gay bar was not a good way to get patrons to stick around.

A woman in her early thirties came out of the back and walked up to them. She was slender, with dark black hair cut short, blue jeans, and a pink and brown sweater that clung to her torso and reached down to her knees.

"Come with me, please," she said.

They followed her into the darkened back room, to a hallway, down this, past the washrooms to an unprepossessing door, which she opened. Her office was small and neat with an electric hurricane lamp on top of a desk with piles of neatly stacked papers. She had a clear plastic phone through which you could see the wires. The walls were painted medium gray. Several tasteful prints of pastoral scenes were framed and hung on each wall. There was a large leather chair behind the modern metallic desk. She motioned for them to sit in the two low-slung leather chairs that faced the desk.

"You didn't think you ruined enough of my business with those first cops? You had to come back?"

"You're the owner?" Fenwick asked.

"I'm Dana Sickles. I'm in charge of what little is left of my clientele. We'd have had a good crowd if your uniformed buddies hadn't been in here harassing my people earlier. I don't break any laws. I do whatever the local commander from the district says. When Ernie the bartender called back here about you two, I called my lawyer. He's on his way. Why am I being hassled?"

"We're investigating a murder."

"Yeah, well so? That's what the other cops said."

"We have reason to believe the victim may have been in your bar."

"Don't give me that crap. Half the planet could have been in here last night. Who would know?"

"Gentleman named Billy Geary who works for you claims he saw him."

"Billy? He shows up on time and is good with the customers. One of the better employees. How'd he know it was him?"

"He goes to law school during the day."

"How does going to law school confer the power of identification?"

"He attended some of the hearings last year on the gay law in Du Page County."

"Good for him. He never bothered to tell me he was going to school, but I get all kinds of different guys here."

Fenwick said, "Tell me about the different kinds."

She glowered at him. "What does that mean?"

"Why do they do it? What's their story?"

"Why do you need to know this?"

"Background. Trying to understand the milieu. We've got a famous person dead. Knowing why he was in your bar, knowing the nature of those working in the bar, could make a difference."

"I don't see how."

Turner said, "If you could please, Ms. Sickles. We're cops trying to solve a murder. We don't want to hassle you. We recognize this is a tremendous inconvenience."

She gave him a skeptical look, but began to answer. "The

boys work here for any number of reason. Essentially for most of them it's because they have low self-esteem."

Turner expressed his astonishment. "Guys who look good enough to be paid money just for twitching have low self-esteem?"

She smiled briefly. "You'd think they'd be on top of the world, but think about it. If you felt positive about yourself, would you need to do this?"

"If I looked that good, I wouldn't mind showing off my body," Fenwick said.

"Maybe for you, but basically these guys need affirmation that they are okay, needed, even loved. Maybe that's why you'd be willing to do it. Maybe that's what you need."

Fenwick smiled. "I'll stick to chocolate. That seems to fulfill a lot of my needs." He showed her the picture of Judge Meade. "You recognize him?"

"You mean do I know what he looks like, or was he in here last night?"

"All of the above," Fenwick said.

"Nope, to all of the above."

"We'll need to talk to everybody who was working here last night."

"Are you nuts?"

"We'd like to do it tonight if at all possible."

She glared at them a moment, then said, "I know I don't have any choice but to cooperate with you, but I'm not happy about this."

The door swung open. Turner thought that being muffled in his overcoat, scarf, hat, and gloves made the man seem more rotund and porcine than he probably was.

"This is my lawyer, Adolf von Steinwehr."

"Don't say anything Dana. You haven't done anything wrong. I'll handle it." He threw off his outer accoutrements. He wore a black business suit, a white shirt, and a red tie. He leaned his butt against the front of the desk almost blocking the view of Dana Sickles behind him. "What's the problem?" he demanded.

Turner said, "Nobody is trying to hassle a gay bar. Nobody is trying to shut this place down. We don't want to arrest anybody connected with the establishment unless they had something to do with the murder of Judge Meade."

"The goddamn prick is dead. Except for lighting bonfires, shooting off fireworks, and having parties, why should we care?"

Fenwick asked, "If he was hated in the gay community, why wouldn't somebody here have reason to murder him?"

"Why here? There's lots of gay establishments in the city."

"We have a witness who says he was here," Turner said.

"Here! Before he was murdered?"

Turner explained about Billy Geary.

Steinwehr looked at Dana. "Who's he?"

"Dancer. Sensible. Never had any problem with him."

"We need to question the employees who were working here last night. We need to know if anybody else saw him, when, what he did, who he was with? You should know the drill."

"You probably don't have a lot of choice, Dana, but I'll stay around to make sure everyone inside isn't strip searched."

Dana said, "Having murder connected with the bar might or might not be good for business, but having cops hovering around the place is a death sentence. You really think you're going to find somebody who saw him?

"We already got one we didn't expect."

"I don't know how much good it's going to do to talk to my employees, but I'll do what I can. Most of them aren't going to want to talk to you."

"Why not?" Fenwick asked.

"The gay ones are going to be suspicious because they're gay and you're cops. Plus they're going to be glad, unlike me, that the judge is dead. The straight ones . . ."

Fenwick interrupted, "The straight ones? Geary mentioned that. At the time, I thought it was odd."

"Yeah, two of my bartenders and a few of the dancers are straight."

"But they all let the guys paw them?" Turner asked.

"You've been here?"

Turner nodded.

She gave him an appraising look. "A gay detective. Are you both?"

"Would it help if we were?" Fenwick asked.

"I don't know. Straight guys, or at least those who say they are, can be just as exhibitionist, just as in need of attention, and just as in need of money as gay men. I pay well. The customers are generous."

"Why are the straight guys not going to want to talk to us?" Fenwick asked.

"You should be able to figure that out. They may work here, put up with the pawing, as you put it, and make decent money, but I bet it's not something they tell their girlfriends or moms and dads."

"Why aren't you glad the judge is dead?" Turner asked.

"I'm a lesbian Republican. I think there are three of us in the country. Talk about endangered species. I agreed with a lot of the judge's decisions. I believe protecting the dignity of the individual should be the highest aim of government. I also think we need lower taxes, less government interference in our lives, and no tax money for abortions. I'll skip the whole list."

"Did you know him?"

"Nope. Never met him. Wouldn't have known him if I passed him on the street."

They called in to Area Ten for a couple of uniformed officers to help them. Sickles worked the phones and called in the employees. Some were reluctant to come in. Turner listened to Sickles's half of the first few conversations and heard her reassure them that the bar's lawyer would be present.

It would be a wait before the first employees showed up so

Turner took the time to drive to pick up Jeff from his overnight trip. While Fenwick waited, he would check the bar carefully. If the killer did the murder in the bar, they doubted if they'd find a convenient spot still covered in blood and gore. They'd probably have to have Crime Lab people in to go over the place.

9

Paul's younger son burbled in the car all the way home. "It was great, Dad. I was better at the video games than everybody except Harold, you know the one who's on my basketball team? He's three years older than me, so I didn't feel too bad losing to him. He took a header in his wheelchair."

"That's terrible," Paul said.

"No, Dad, it was funny. He's such a jerk and a show-off. He was trying to do a wheelie. Two of the adults saw what he was trying to do and tried to stop him but they were too late."

"They should have been supervising more closely."

"We're not helpless, Dad. I told you about the wheelchair races we have. It's cool."

Paul made appropriate parental warning noises about Jeff racing in his wheelchair. Jeff had been bugging Paul to let him join some of the outdoor races in the summer where wheelchairs were allowed. Paul suspected he was going to say yes, eventually. He knew once he said yes, Jeff would probably begin lobbying for a modified, racing wheelchair. Turner asked more about the sleep-over, and Jeff talked excitedly on.

Jeff had the birth defect spina bifida. That meant that at birth his spinal cord and nerves protruded in a sac from his back, near the bottom of his spine. He was born with bladder and bowel dysfunction and paralysis of his legs. Except for a brief scare a year before, when his shunt had to be unclogged, there had been no major health problems in recent years.

Paul drove up to Mrs. Talucci's house. He had called her before he left the bar. Rose Talucci lived next door to the Turners. She had the ground floor of the house to herself. On the second floor lived Mrs. Talucci's two daughters and several distant female cousins. At ninety-two, Mrs. Talucci ruled this brood, her main concern being to keep them out of her way and to stay independent. Numerous times she'd confided in Paul that if they weren't family, she'd throw them all out. She did her own cooking, cleaning, and shopping, as she had for seventy-four years. To her daughters' horror, she took the bus, El, or subway on her own throughout the city and even to suburbs to visit friends, relatives, attend shopping-center openings or anything else that struck her fancy. Paul loved Rose. She cared for Jeff after school whenever Paul or Brian couldn't be home, and often wound up giving the boys and their dad dinner. This was prearranged on a weekly basis. For several years after it started, she refused all offers of payment. Being neighbors and having known Paul and his family since before he was born, precluded even discussing such things. But one day Mrs. Talucci couldn't fix a broken porch. Paul had offered, and since then he'd done all repairs and had even made several major renovations on her home.

A few weeks ago, she'd been diagnosed with cancer. She had refused treatments, which the doctor said would almost certainly be painful and debilitating, and, at her age, wouldn't prolong her life much anyway. She insisted that the quality of her remaining time was what was important, not prolonging her ninety-two years. The only significant change she'd permitted in her lifestyle was that she didn't organize the Christmas dinner for her family. She announced at Thanksgiving she was going to Bermuda for the holiday. She'd taken a week-long cruise that included a three-day stay on the island. She'd returned two days ago with a magnificent tan. She claimed she pinched the butt of her steward just for the hell of it.

Mrs. Talucci answered the door and hurried them inside.

She offered to give Paul dinner, but he told her he had to get back to work.

"I heard Judge Meade died," she said.

"Buck and I have the case."

"Almost wish I'd read more law when I went back to school. Never saw much point in it. Didn't want to argue with a bunch of morons. I did read a few of his decisions."

"You did?"

"He was against everything I was for. I try to keep up. I found the reasoning in what he wrote good, if you accepted his basic premises."

"I heard he was stupid."

"Could have been. It usually says who writes the decisions. Maybe his clerks wrote them for him or something. Seemed about average-bright to me."

After her husband had died over twenty years ago, Rose had started back to school. She graduated magna cum laude from three different universities, accumulating one bachelor's and two master's degrees. She was proudest of her degree in philosophy from the University of Chicago.

Paul stopped at his own house to call Ben, who had already planned to stay the night at Paul's. Ben offered to pick up Jeff later from Mrs. Talucci's. Paul appreciated the offer.

10

When Turner got back to Au Naturel, only five employees had showed up, but Sickles had managed to get hold of over ninety percent of them. A steady stream of some of the most attractive men in town began trickling into the bar.

Before they got started, Fenwick took Turner on a brief tour of the premises.

"I know you're familiar with this place," Fenwick said. "I checked around in back. I found nothing suspicious. I think the back doorway should be gone over carefully. There is no blood anywhere on the pavement out back. Not sure how you'd clean it without the cleanser itself freezing. Unless you had a personal blow torch you happen to bring along with your gun when you're doing murders."

"Could be all the rage with killers."

"You ever been through this whole place?"

"I've been waiting for your guided tour."

The dancers' dressing room looked like a high school locker room for the overly butch: skimpy, slinky, filthy, sweaty, smelly clothes were strewn on most every surface. The lighting ran to the more lurid shades of pink and purple. There were a series of small offices behind Dana Sickles'. No windows were large enough to shove a body through. Nothing leapt out at them and said, "Hi, I'm a clue."

Over the next hour, what the police basically did was show

each person the picture of the judge, then ask if they'd seen him last night. All of them that Turner and Fenwick talked to were solemnly quiet. Each looked at the picture. Some looked thoughtful before answering. They all gave the same answer—none had seen the judge.

Only a few said they remembered Billy's announcement about the judge being in the bar. On such a busy night it was possible for a dancer to make over a hundred dollars during each set for only a few minutes of bumping and grinding. Their thoughts were concentrated on that. The few who remembered what he said hadn't seen the judge and didn't know what he looked like anyway.

Turner and Fenwick took down all their names and asked Sickles for the names and addresses of those whom they had been unable to interview.

They got done just after nine. A brief walk in the cold got them to their car.

"Must be at least twenty below zero," Turner said.

"Know what really fries my socks about this weather?" Fenwick asked as he started the car.

"Long winter underwear sticking to your crotch."

"Hey, you're good."

"You told me that earlier."

"Sounds like me. I mean in addition to that."

"I'm paralyzed with anticipation. When I woke up this morning, I said to myself, I hope Buck tells me more about his long winter underwear."

"Jealous?"

"Only in my wildest nightmare."

Fenwick said, "It's two more things really, well, three."

"Get on with it."

"First, the lack of heat in these cars. Second, the glee in the weather forecasters' voices as they predict new record lows. But the worst is when they tell us to bundle up. As if the television and radio forecasters have become our mothers. They just get done telling us it's a million degrees below zero, and then they tell us to 'bundle up.' How stupid do they think we are?"

"How many times have we been faced with the stupidest criminals in the country, and the next day they do something even dumber?"

"And then we get Carruthers."

"See," Turner said, "they're performing a valuable service."

"We done for the day?"

"Just the commander and any other brass who happen to want to stick their nose in this. A stack of reports to get started. Plans for tomorrow."

"Well, shit. That's nothing. We should eat first."

They stopped at Ed Debevic's on Ontario Street for a burger. Turner hated the place. He found the fifties-sassy-waitress schtick tiring. Buck loved it. He found flirting with the waitresses enjoyable. Turner figured it was a heterosexual thing. He was willing to indulge his partner once in a while since the food was good. They managed to see the last twenty seconds of one football game.

The "nothing" they had left to do took them well over two hours. Reporting to everyone and beginning reports got them no closer to a killer but, tired as they were, they made sure that what they wrote and what they said was as accurate as possible. You didn't want to mess up your case with any kind of slip-up. No one wanted their face plastered on national television for screwing up an investigation.

11

Ian's call came in around eleven o'clock, just as Turner was typing his notes from the conversation with Mrs. Meade.

"Thanks for the tip," Turner said.

"You learn anything else?"

"No. Only your buddy Billy saw him. You sure 'Buddy Billy' is reliable?"

"You talked to him, what do you think?"

"You've slept with him, you know him better than I do."

"Sleeping with someone confers wisdom?"

"You slept with me and look at where it got you."

"All this and heaven too. Well, sweet cakes, I've got another one for you."

"How come we aren't finding this stuff? I don't like coincidences, Ian."

"I've got better sources in the gay community than you do. I know who to talk to. Remember, you're speaking with the man who knows deep dish on everybody. The gay community in this town isn't that big. All I ever do is say, 'my, how interesting, tell me more,' and they do. Not my fault everybody loves to blab. Besides, who do you know that's nosier or more bold than I?"

"Somewhere on the planet there must be someone."

"Ha. Knew you couldn't think of anybody. I've got my original source. He's willing to talk."

"He's more reliable now than he was earlier?"

"Well, no."

"It's late. If this is nothing, I'd rather wait until morning. I enjoy 'nothing' in the morning more than I do at night."

"Your decision. I'd be happy to be the one to solve the case based on what this guy says."

Turner looked at his watch and sighed. "I'm beat, but with a case like this I'm not sure I've got much choice."

"I don't recommend waiting. He's pretty skittish. He could change his mind by the time you got down here."

"Did this one know Billy Geary?"

"Billy says he never heard of this kid. I don't know. My source heard they were calling in all the employees of Au Naturel to talk to. He doesn't work there, but he was in the bar and in the dancers' dressing room."

"So he could have good information?" Turner asked.

"Maybe. I just want to emphasize going easy. I think he's the skipping-town type."

"Why would he leave town?"

"He has no roots here. He gets hassled, he just ups and leaves."

"Swell. Is he of age?"

"He was in the bar, so he's got to be at least twenty-one, right?"

"I guess."

He agreed to meet Ian at the paper. Turner explained all this to Fenwick who said, "All the football games are over. Might as well make the night a total washout."

Planning to go straight home after this interview, they drove their own cars.

Ian met them in the downstairs entryway of the paper. Most of the lights in the building were off. Ian's face was half in shadow as he talked to them.

"Is he still here?" Turner asked.

"Yeah, but I wanted to remind you to be extra gentle with this one."

"And why is that?" Fenwick asked. "Not that I don't believe in sweetness and light."

"He's a basket case."

"I was thinking to myself on the way over," Fenwick said, "that what this case needed is a raving loon."

"Why is he a basket case?" Turner asked.

"As soon as I heard about Meade's death, I knew it was going to be a big story. I've tried for years to get an interview with him. I've rarely gotten much beyond the switchboard at the Kennedy Federal Building. At his talks I've gone to, I've tried to ask my questions. He learned to spot me pretty quick. After a while, he'd just smile at me and go on to the next question. Eventually his handlers would escort me out. The last few years they wouldn't even let me in the door."

"I presume all this has something to do with our delicate friend?"

"I take that kind of brush-off as a challenge. I got to know all kinds of people working in the federal court system. I planted the kid you're about to meet in the mail room."

"You've got that kind of clout?" Turner asked.

"I dated the man who hires and fires in the mail room."

"Just to get someone in?"

"Heavens, you offend me."

"Which means I was right."

"The kid needed a job. Mostly he lives on the streets. Hustling isn't the most secure profession. I happened to know somebody who could help."

"So, the kid is a homeless waif, and he worked in the mail room. I know there's a point to this somewhere."

"He knew the judge. He never got me any useful information. He got fired for being an incompetent boob, which he is pretty much."

"But you've taken him under your wing and . . ."

"And I've given him the benefit of my extensive experience."

"So why are we talking to him?"

"He says he saw the judge last night, but there might be

more to it. I'll let you guys talk to him. If nothing else, he'll confirm the judge's presence in the bar, but he's hinted he knows more than that."

"What?" Turner asked.

"He's going to have to tell you. He won't tell me."

"I thought your charm worked on everybody."

"I wasn't trying to seduce him. I just want him to talk."

Ian led the way up the stairs and down the hall to his office. The heat must have been turned down for the evening, because Turner could feel tendrils of cold.

"Sorry, they turn the heat off after ten every night. It's usually pretty comfortable. With this much cold . . ." Ian shook his head.

A kid who looked barely to be out of his middle teens sat at Ian's computer playing chess. He stood up as they entered. Ian introduced him as Carl Schurz.

His handshake was cold and clammy. He barely glanced at either of the two cops. His eyes roved around the room, as if waiting for monsters to seep out of the woodwork. His arms seemed to be in movement every moment with limp wrists and a bone structure that suggested not one of his muscles had ever done anything more difficult than lift a feather. When he sat back down, either his foot tapped on the floor or the fingers on one hand or the other drummed on the arm of a chair or on the computer keyboard. Some part of his body seemed to be constantly fluttering nervously.

He was scarecrow-thin in faded blue jeans, a flannel shirt that hung past his knees, and black running shoes.

He sat back down. His hand went to his mouth. He looked from Turner to the computer screen, then Fenwick, Ian and finally back to Turner.

"You can't ever tell anyone you've seen me," the kid began.

"I don't know what your story is," Turner said. "If I can help you, I will. I have no desire to bring trouble to you."

"I'm nineteen. Ian's tried to get me several jobs. I can't do them right. People get angry. I wish I could . . ."

Turner leaned against the same wall he had hours earlier. Carl sat in the chair. Next to the computer, Ian stood facing the kid. Fenwick planted his bulk almost directly behind the kid. Four people in the small room made the atmosphere seem exceptionally close.

Carl said, "You frighten me."

"Why is that?" Turner asked.

"Both of you are big and strong. You could hurt me if you wanted to. Ian said you wouldn't hurt me. He said you were gay. Are you really a gay cop? Are you both gay?"

"I'm a gay police detective."

"I saw something last night."

"What did you see?"

"I know there are places in the Kennedy Federal Building in the Loop where you can't be found. I never tell anyone else because they might try and horn in on me. I've kept my identification from when I worked there. I know computer codes. I watched how the building works. I know some of the people who work there. They're really nice to me."

"What did you see?" Turner asked again.

The kid shivered as if he were outside in the twenty-below weather.

"Are you all right?" Turner asked.

"Yes, yes, yes."

"Do you take drugs?" Turner asked.

"No."

"What did you want to tell me?"

"I'm a great piano player. I have an IQ over a zillion. I watch and observe everything. Nobody believes I graduated from high school. Education on this side of the Atlantic is so screwed up. I knew I should have stayed in Paris."

At this moment Turner joined him in this last sentiment, unless, of course, he supplied a clue to the murder, or better yet confessed on the spot. The nineteen-year-old shifted his position in Ian's chair so both legs were pulled under his scrawny butt.

Fenwick said, "You're very bright. You studied in Europe. You worked in the Kennedy Federal Building. Fascinating. Don't let us stop you."

"You don't have to be sarcastic," Schurz said.

"Why did you tell Ian you saw Judge Meade in the bar last night?" Turner asked.

"Oh, that. I was in the dressing room when Billy made the announcement."

Ian shouted, "All you heard was the announcement? You didn't actually see him?"

"Wait!" Carl said. "I . . . just listen." The kid wrapped his arms around his lean torso. Turner noted the nearly fleshless wrists.

"You were nineteen and working there?" Turner asked.

"No. I was visiting a friend."

"Who?"

"I don't want to tell you his name."

"Did you actually see the judge?" Turner asked.

"I'm cold."

"Are you on drugs now?" Turner asked.

"No, no, no."

Fenwick bashed his hand against the filing cabinet he stood next to. The kid jumped. "What the fuck is this?" Fenwick growled. "It's cold. It's late. I haven't had my after-dinner snack, and you've got a chance of being it if you don't cut the shit."

The kid burst into tears.

Fenwick said, "All right, you're under arrest for being a sniveling idiot. Hold out your hands."

The kid added deep, heart-wrenching sobs to his crying.

Turner spoke very softly. "Carl, did you kill Judge Meade?"

Carl snuffled, drew a deep breath, and squeaked out, "No," and resumed bawling.

"I'll be dipped," Fenwick muttered. He turned to Ian. "You got coffee in this place?"

"Some instant stuff in a kitchenette down on the second floor."

"I'll be back," Fenwick said. "If either of you strangles him while I'm gone, I'll testify that you were in Barbados when it happened."

Fenwick's absence diminished the occupied space in the room considerably.

The kid wiped snot on his sleeve. Ian handed him a box of tissues. Carl unlimbered his legs, sat up straight, and dabbed at his face.

Turner let the silence continue as Carl composed himself. Finally the kid said, "Is that other guy coming back?"

"Yes," Turner said.

"I won't talk. I want to leave."

Turner shifted his position so that his butt rested on the edge of Ian's desk. He put his hand gently on Carl's. He waited until the kid's eyes met his. "I need you to help me. Gay people have to stick together. If you can do something to help me find the killer, I would really appreciate it. We don't have any clues right now. You could be the key to solving the whole thing."

The kid's leg moved so that it brushed Turner's and stayed resting against his calf.

Turner glanced up at Ian. Ian shrugged. Turner couldn't tell if the physical contact was accidental, a mild attempt at seduction, or a yearning for human warmth. He moved his leg so the contact was barely noticeable.

"I'd like to hear what you have to say," Turner said.

"I want to tell this my way," Carl said.

"I'm here to listen."

"You won't let that other one hurt me?"

"No."

"Someone like him raped me when I was nine." For the second time Carl's eyes met Turner's. "I haven't had a good night's sleep since. When I was thirteen, I tried to rape my little brother and my little sister. I've been to lots of therapists. I tried suicide three times. I didn't have the nerve to finish myself. I ran away from home several times before I was even in high school. The last time I ran away I was sixteen. My parents didn't try to find me. I met Ian. He was pretty nice to me. He didn't try to have sex with me. Most everybody else who wanted to help me demanded something in return."

"How old are you really?"

The kid looked down at the floor. He mumbled, "Seventeen."

Carl's leg was now comfortably resting against Turner's. The detective moved his farther away.

Carl's face was red from his crying, but he'd ceased to breathe heavily. He held onto a tissue in one hand.

Paul said, "Tell me about knowing what the judge looked like."

"The Federal Building job Ian got for me was nice, but I'm not very good at things. I'm really bright. I don't want you to think I'm stupid. I'm not. I did study in Europe for a year. I just can't seem to concentrate. If I ever studied I got all A's. I tried lots of jobs. I always get fired."

Fenwick returned to the room. He held a cup of coffee.

The kid sat up straighter and pulled out another tissue from the box.

"I don't want him here," Carl said.

Fenwick smiled, said, "My pleasure," and left. Turner and Fenwick had played the roles of good cop/bad cop for years. Fenwick might not know exactly what was going on, but the lack of cues from Turner to stay was sufficient for him to know it was best to leave the questioning to Turner.

Carl now had a sense of power and a little more confidence as he spoke. "Like I said, I learned all the secrets of the Federal Building. I know a lot of places in the Loop that throw the homeless out as soon as they step in the door, but I've slept in most of them. You've got to be smart, resourceful, and sometimes willing to put out. Is that okay to tell you?"

The kid shifted the swivel chair enough so his knee came into contact with Turner's knee. This time Turner let the contact linger for a few moments. To move casually away it was necessary for him to move his butt on the desk. If the kid kept this up, Turner would soon fall off the end.

"I'm not here to get you in trouble," Turner said.

"Last night I went to the Federal Building. I kind of hang out there. One of the older security guards, he's got a wife, two kids, and three grandkids, but he likes to fool around once in a while. His closet is my key to a warm night."

"What's the name of the security guard?"

"I can't tell you. He's been good to me."

They'd check it out the next day.

"So what happened?"

"I was waiting for my friend in one of the guard rooms. I heard voices outside the room. I got a little scared because only my buddy was supposed to be on duty. I scrunched down behind the console. I could hear everything they said. They were arguing, sounded like they'd been at it for a while. At one point one of them said, 'Well, so, Judge Meade won't be so high and mighty after this." I moved around so I could peek out the door. I could see Judge Meade plainly. When I worked for Ian, I made sure I knew the basic things he wanted. At least I did that right when I worked there."

"You're sure it was Judge Meade?"

"Absolutely. No doubt."

"Nobody else heard them?"

"It's a big building. I wasn't supposed to be where I was."

"Did you recognize who he was with?"

"That was the bizarre thing. I thought I heard three voices, but I only saw two guys. My angle wasn't very good. Judge Meade said something I couldn't hear and then the other guy raised his hand as if to hit him. He was cursing and yelling. The judge didn't flinch, but the guy stopped short of hitting him. He turned around and ran off."

"You get a good look at him?"

"Yeah."

"Did you recognize him?"

"Not then."

"What happened next?"

"The judge left like he was in a hurry. My buddy came down and I took care of him. He gives himself a treat every holiday. Since it was New Year's Eve, and I said I wanted to go out for a while, he didn't mind. It's not like he's got a crush on me. I'm an outlet for him. So I went to Au Naturel to meet a friend."

"What happened there?"

"It was crazy. I went to the dressing room because my friend is one of the dancers. What I saw was the guy from the Federal Building. The one who was going to hit the judge was one of the dancers."

"Did he say or do anything when Billy made his announcement?"

"He didn't react either way. I remember he was putting on a chain harness that I thought made him look really hot. He didn't do anything. I asked my friend who he was. He didn't know. My buddy just started working there. A lot of the guys are part time, and they don't usually work there that long."

"Describe him for me."

"About six feet tall. Sort of reddish-blond hair. Flat stomach. Huge pecs. Red thong."

"What'd he wear at the Federal Building?"

"Long trench coat and jeans. I'm telling mostly what I remember from seeing him when he was dancing."

"Did you see the judge in the bar?"

"Once, just before midnight. This guy I was telling you about was dancing and the judge was in a corner staring at him. I was distracted with my friends and partying, so I didn't pay much attention. At the time I didn't care much. I knew Judge Meade was homophobic from what Ian said, but I knew I had a warm place to stay for the night, and I was having a good time. I guess I just thought, here's another self-hating homosexual. I hate myself a lot of the time, so I thought I understood. He's got to be a horrible closet case."

"Shouldn't be hard to get the name of the dancer," Ian said.

Turner nodded agreement. "None of the ones we interviewed mentioned the judge. Of course, the killer would be understandably hesitant to bring it up. We'll go back and look at the employee list. Would you be willing to look at the dancers and tell me which one it was?"

Carl hesitated.

"Please," Turner said, "it would really help."

Carl smiled and rested his hand on Turner's. "Sure," he said, "if it'll help."

The logistics for the rest of the evening were for Carl to sleep on the couch at Ian's. Turner and Fenwick would go to their respective homes and they would all meet again at nine in the morning to begin trying to identify the dancing boy in question.

Ian said, "I need to talk to Detective Turner for a minute, Carl. Could you wait down at the front door?"

"Sure." Carl hesitated. He got out of the chair and stood in front of Turner. Carl whispered, "Would you hold me?"

Turner hesitated.

The boy murmured, "Just for a second. Please. I'm frightened."

Turner stood up and embraced him gently. Carl's return hug was fierce and demanding. Turner felt the youth's trembling ease. He felt bad for the youngster, but the kid had more needs than Turner wanted to meet even if he could. The kid was a therapist's nightmare. Turner also reminded himself that he was a cop and this was a possible suspect. He allowed the embrace for a few moments then carefully disengaged himself. Carl hurried out of the room.

"I hope Fenwick doesn't eat him," Ian said.

"Poor kid is a mess," Turner said. "Where did you find him?"

"Meeting some needs of my own."

"He said you hadn't had sex."

"Not with someone that young and vulnerable. He brings out a lot of paternal instincts in me. He's been badly bruised. Being a gay kid is tough enough. A raped and brutalized one has got to be a million times worse. I just hope I can help enough so he doesn't try to off himself again."

"What was that hug about at the end?" Turner asked.

"I'm not sure. I saw the knee thing. I thought he might end up sitting in your lap."

"I don't need a gay teenager on my hands."

"You handled it fine."

"Do I believe everything he's told me? Should I believe everything he told me?"

"I don't have reason to doubt it, yet."

"Which is not the same as believing him."

Fenwick opened the door and poked his head in. "Is it safe?"

Turner nodded.

"Anything useful?" Fenwick asked.

Turner filled him in and finished with, "We've heard his side of his terrible life. What the truth is might be hard to decipher. His parents could be sweet people, pining away in front of some suburban fireplace for all we know."

Fenwick commented, "Creep, asshole, or holy terror, what he gave us has some possibilities. Whether or not he can identify the dancer, we've got the film from the camera at the Federal Building."

"Gives another focus point on the judge that night. This is two I owe you Ian."

"Does this mean our Judge Meade, homophobe extraordinaire, was a closet-case deluxe?" Ian asked.

"You swallow a dictionary?" Fenwick asked.

"Sure looks like he is," Turner said. "Maybe somebody was going to out him?"

"A ripe case for it," Fenwick said, "but I thought that 'outing' was kind of passé."

"It is and it isn't," Ian said. "I'd love to be the one to out Judge Meade, but the paper doesn't publish again for another week. I'm not sure we've got absolute certainty, but it sure looks more than fishy to me. Inhabiting a gay dance bar on New Year's Eve. Meeting with one of the 'dancers' prior to, sounds like an assignation to me. I'm going to wait until I can talk to someone who knows more. Somebody who went to bed with him could convince me. Being at a gay bar or talking to a hot young man doesn't quite meet my criteria for being gay. I need a little more."

Turner said, "If he met the guy earlier, why go to the bar and risk being seen? Does a severe closet case go to a bar?"

"Does a straight judge pick a gay bar to party in on New Year's Eve when he's supposed to be in Montreal?"

"Lots of questions to be answered," Turner said.

"This closet crap is such bullshit," Ian said.

"How so?" Fenwick asked.

"Hiding in this day and age, by these kinds of people, is silly."

Turner kept his annoyance in check. He and Ian had discussed levels of closetedness before. Years before, Turner's insistence on keeping silent about himself at work had led to their break up as lovers. He would live an open life to those closest to him whom he could trust. He'd come out more each year.

Usually Ian and Turner avoided the subject of how out it was politically correct to be. Ian occasionally made cracks as he had just done. Turner wasn't sure if he did it to irritate him deliberately, or if it was just a comment he was used to making. Turner didn't much respect someone who crowed about the importance of coming out, if that person, like Ian, worked in a job surrounded by gay people. Ian was also out to his parents and safely indifferent to any negative reactions. For now he let the crack slide. Ian could still piss him off faster than anybody but his own parents or his sons. That was the price you paid for being good friends with an ex-lover.

Oblivious to these nuances, Fenwick said, "Your buddy Carl was weird."

Ian said, "I wanted to talk to you with him out of the room. I want to emphasize again the need to go easy on the kid. I know you guys do your act real well. Remember, this is a bright kid. He's sensitive, fragile, and suicidal. He probably opened up more for Paul because of what you did, Buck, but just go easy on him."

"You in love?" Fenwick asked.

"You two aren't the only ones allowed to have paternal feelings."

"What else can you tell me about Dana Sickles?" Turner asked.

"Smart, smart businesswoman, a Republican. Has a little gold mine in Au Naturel."

"She mentioned she's a lesbian Republican," Turner said.

"Isn't that an oxymoron?" Fenwick asked.

"Gay and lesbian Republicans are to the right on economic issues, and also believe in privacy, hence many of them think gay people don't even need laws protecting them, since the right to privacy is sacrosanct."

"They really believe that?" Fenwick asked.

"Claim they do," Ian said.

Turner said, "Let me get this straight; after the budget is balanced, taxes are lowered, and the poor are in their place—they believe the right wing is just going to leave us alone? Are they on the same planet with the rest of us?"

Ian said, "They'll have their goddamn money, and they can spend it all the way to the concentration camps. She believes in money for herself—a policy of enlightened self-interest. Me first, money first. Their attitude is, if I've got enough money, no one can hurt me. Some of you poor slobs with real jobs, non–gay community jobs, may lose them, but she'll have a balanced budget."

Turner said, "I don't have a lot of time for politics tonight. Let's get your friend Carl tucked in bed and get moving. It's late."

On the way downstairs, Turner asked, "Dana have problems with the bar? Police hassles? Community jealousy?"

"Everything is supposed to be just fabulous. My sources, which are superb, say this is true. She has lots of friends. As you can attest to personally, her bar is very popular. I'm going to dig deeper. I assume the judge was there for closeted reasons, but I want to find out as much as I can about that place."

When they got to the first floor, they couldn't find Carl. The other employees of the paper had long since departed. They searched all three floors of the building carefully. They met back in the entryway.

Ian shook his head. "He's definitely gone."

They gazed at each other for a few moments.

Then Fenwick spoke. "I'll ask the question. Why did the sniveling little creep run?"

"Scared?" Ian said. "Changed his mind? He was lying all the time? Remembered an important appointment with his dentist? Kidnapped by aliens? How the hell should I know?"

"He's your witness," Turner pointed out.

"Yeah, well, he might be the key to your case," Ian said.

"Or maybe not," Fenwick said.

"Or maybe not," Ian agreed.

"Look," Turner said, "I appreciate the call and the information. I agree with you, he is unreliable, and I would not be eager to get him onto a witness stand. I think a competent attorney could rip him to shreds."

"Should we stop at Au Naturel tonight?" Fenwick asked.

"It's worth a try," Turner said. "The kid has a head start on us. He could be sorry for what he said, or maybe he's running to warn somebody. I'd like to get to the bar and check this out, if we can."

The three of them drove to Au Natural and parked one behind the other in a loading zone directly in front of the bar.

Inside, the place was completely quiet. The music was muted. Two guys sat at the bar. The dancer stood with his hand on his hips watching one of the television screens. The owner wasn't there. No one had seen Carl. Neither the bartender nor the patrons would admit to knowing of anyone who fit Carl's description, nor that of the mystery dancer. The two detectives and the reporter decided to call it a night.

At home, Paul found Ben at the kitchen table reading the book *The Gay Militants* by Donn Teal. Paul kissed his lover and asked, "Is Jeff asleep?"

Ben nodded.

Paul looked in on his younger son. Jeff slept quietly. Paul rearranged the covers, leaned over, and placed a gentle kiss on his son's forehead.

Upstairs in the bedroom, Ben said, "Brian called. He said they were going to Disney World even though they didn't win the Super Bowl. He said he wanted to go to Key West tomorrow so he could bring us back a gay souvenir. Sounded like he was having an excellent time."

"Good for him."

"He also razzed me about the cold. He told me to make sure to keep you warm at night and be sure that you dressed warm when you went out."

"Just what I need, a teenage mother."

"He ended by saying happy New Year."

"They're an hour ahead of us. I'll try and call him tomorrow morning before I leave for work."

"You might wake him up."

"He'll live."

Paul took out the pager he'd brought that day. He showed it to Ben and wrote down the number and gave it to him. Finally they tumbled into bed. Paul snuggled close to Ben, felt his lover's arms go around him. He breathed deeply and contentedly.

12

The next morning, showered and shaved, Paul made his way downstairs. He found Jeff in the kitchen reading *Freddy and the Flying Saucer Plans* by Walter R. Brooks. Without looking up from the book, Jeff said, "Your turn to cook breakfast, Dad."

Paul hugged his son then began rummaging in the refrigerator. Ben appeared and also gave Jeff a hug—Paul was extremely pleased at how well his sons got along with Ben.

Breakfast was an important time in the Turner household. Paul insisted he and his sons have a cooked meal to start the day. With schedules so varied and Paul's work so demanding, they often missed each other the rest of the day. They took turns cooking and cleaning. Ben had been staying over often enough now that he'd joined the breakfast cooking rotation.

Jeff's breakfasts were still a little simpler than the others, both because he was younger and because of his dependence on his crutches. Still, Paul preferred Jeff's breakfasts to Brian's. His older son had been on a health kick for several years now. As an athlete, he felt compelled to keep his body in as perfect a shape as possible. He seldom discouraged his older son's fanaticism, but this morning he was pleased to know there would be no unnamed vegetables lurking in his eggs.

After breakfast, Paul called Brian's hotel room. He was surprised when a female voice answered. When the person found out who was calling, she became quite flustered. She said, "He's in the shower, he's not here, oh, wait." After several seconds of silence, he heard distant banging on a door, then a muffled, "Brian, it's the phone. It's your dad. He probably thinks I spent the night. I hope I didn't get you in trouble."

Several minutes of silence, a few thumping footsteps, then, "Hi, dad."

"Having a coed sleep-over?"

"Dad, José and I are sharing a room. The chaperones check every night."

"Every three hours?"

"Well, no."

"Who is she?"

"The coach's daughter. She was just here picking up a spare-room key she forgot."

They both said, "How convenient," at the same time.

"Do I want to know why you had her spare-room key or would it be best at this time to be discreet?"

"You want pictures or written descriptions?"

"Neither." They talked for ten minutes. Brian sounded happy and like he was having a good time. As any parent, he hoped his boy had good sense, or at least used a condom, but with a seventeen-year-old much of the time you could only hope you had brought him up right.

Ben and Paul returned to Paul's after depositing Jeff at Mrs. Talucci's.

Paul said, "We interviewed a gay teenager yesterday." He told Ben about Carl Schurz.

Ben listened carefully. "The kid affected you."

"Yeah, he's a suspect and all, but I know what it was like to be a messed-up gay teen. It wasn't nearly as bad for me as it is for him. I felt sorry for him. I wish I could have been more help than just a hug."

"Sometimes that's all you can give."

Paul kissed and held his lover and then left for work.

* * *

After roll call at headquarters, Turner and Fenwick met with Roosevelt, Wilson, and Acting Commander Molton. They compared notes and talked about courses of action.

Fenwick said, "Everybody will be working at the Kennedy Federal Building today. We've got uniforms to do the most peripheral folks. Paul and I should be able to interview all the people who came into contact with Meade daily. Might be something there. We can also requisition that tape and talk to some security guards."

Turner said, "Carl Schurz wouldn't give us the name, but it won't be that hard to find out who was on duty. They must keep records."

Molton said, "We'll have a list of court cases the judge ruled on down here by the end of the morning, along with all of his written decisions. Don't know how that's going to help, but it might. I don't envy you having to wade through all that legal crap, but you'll probably have to."

"Maybe we could get a legal scholar to sum it up for us," Fenwick said.

"Detailed summary is fine," Molton said, "but what if you miss something by not having read it yourself?"

"We'll get the summary, then see what we need to go through," Turner said.

Molton agreed to let them assign someone to the task. "I've got some gossip on the judges," Molton said. "An old lawyer friend of mine filled me in. Supposedly, these federal judges who make around $120,000 a year are jealous of lawyers who, of course, make much more."

"They make more than all of us," Wilson said.

"It is not unheard of for them to step down and take a position with a law firm where they can make far more money. My source also says they can be very lonely. Attorneys worry about being seen with them."

"I worry about being seen with lawyers," Roosevelt said.

"That's prejudiced," Fenwick said.

Molton continued, "I've got a sort of cynical source. He claims that their decisions are often capricious and arbitrary."

"He said capricious and arbitrary?" Fenwick asked.

"He's a lawyer," Molton responded. "He claimed that they often listen to a case, and then decide it on whether or not they've voted for somebody from that law firm recently."

"Renews my faith in the judiciary," Turner said.

"That's all I have," Molton said.

Roosevelt and Wilson gave their final report on the canvass of the neighborhood. "You got one possible at the end of the block," Wilson said. "Owner of a used bookstore which is going broke. He was working in the back of his store early that morning. Claims he might have heard something."

Turner wrote down the name and address.

"We'll call Dana Sickles and get over to the bar as soon as it opens," Turner said. "We could use some help finding the disappearing Carl Schurz."

Roosevelt and Wilson promised to do what they could.

"We need to stop at Judge Meade's house," Turner said. "We haven't found his appointment book or his luggage. Plus maybe his kids will be home. We've got to talk to them."

Molton said, "I'm holding a press conference soon. We've got a fair number of reporters sniffing around."

Fenwick said, "They won't get bored with this one anytime soon."

"Got that right," Molton said.

On the third floor, two men in dark-blue business suits sat at Turner and Fenwick's desks. Fenwick's eyes lit up like a starving grizzly bear's at the sight of a fresh salmon buffet.

As Fenwick lumbered forward, the two men got to their feet. One held out his hand and said, "I'm Special Agent John Smith, this is Special Agent Joe Brown."

"This is a joke," Fenwick said.

Smith gave him a puzzled look. "We're here to offer you any

help we can with the case. We don't know if the Bureau needs to be involved or not."

"You're here to waste our time," Fenwick said.

Smith sighed. "The sooner you fill us in, the sooner we leave."

Fenwick plucked six different folders from the top of his desk. Each bulged with paper. "Someone will make copies of these for you and then you can read them and leave them here. It's everything we've got."

"Thanks for your cooperation," Brown said.

"Have a nice day," Fenwick said. "Drop dead. Go to Hell," he muttered when they were out of ear shot.

As they walked through the first floor to sign out a car, Carruthers waved from the far end of the hall and hurried toward them. Three-quarters of the way there, he was intercepted by Rodriguez. "Let's leave the real detectives alone," Rodriguez said.

Carruthers began a protest. Rodriguez put a firm grip on Carruthers' arm and pulled him away. Turner heard Rodriguez say, "We've got a dead gang-banger, Randy. You like those kinds of cases."

They called the chief of security at the Kennedy Federal Building to alert her to their arrival. They phoned Judge Wadsworth's office and told the secretary they'd be in to interview Meade's staff that morning.

They met the head of security in her office. She was a woman in her late forties with a Doris Day pixieishness about her. Turner thought it might be the freckles or the bright smile. Her name was Janice Caldwell.

They explained about the lapse by the security guard and about the need for the film from New Year's Eve.

She did not look the slightest bit pixieish on hearing the news of the breach of security. "Let me check my list," she said immediately. She tapped on a computer keyboard, gazed at the screen for a moment. "It was Leo. I knew it. I just checked to be sure. He's the only one who was working that night who would meet the description you gave me. I'll call and get him down here." She agreed to process the film as quickly as possible. She also checked with Judge Wadsworth so they could begin questioning those who had worked with Judge Meade.

They were alone in the elevator to the judge's office. Fenwick began singing, "We've got suspects, we've got lots and lots of suspects."

"You're singing again, Buck, and it's not Broadway show tunes. I'm worried."

"Just all aquiver with excitement about meeting all these new folks."

They dumped their winter coats, scarves, gloves, and hats on the chairs in the judge's office and began their interviews.

First was his secretary, Blanche Dussenberg. She was a brightly pink woman, as if her face had been stuck outside in the bitter cold too long, or she'd dunked her entire face in a vat of bright pink blush. She wore a multihued designer scarf, a brown dress, and sensible black oxfords. She carried a box of tissues.

After introductions they got her settled.

Turner said, "We need some basic information, Ms. Dussenberg. How the office ran, how people got along, who did what."

"Judge Meade was a wonderful man. He was kind, thoughtful, always pleasant to those who worked under him."

One of the cop truisms is that you seldom learned anything useful from people closest to the victim. Those who were near and dear tended to be friends and care about the deceased, otherwise they wouldn't be called close. You looked for the neighborhood gossip, the office tattletale, the one with the grudge who was willing to give the cheap, tawdry gossip. That person might give a hint, drop a bit of history, a snippet of knowledge that might lead to a clue or at least something interesting. All they got from Blanche was friendly, tear-spattered, chatter about how wonderful the place and Judge Meade were.

After listening to fifteen minutes of basic office data, Turner asked her about the judge's appointment book. She went to her desk and returned. "This is only my copy. He keeps his at home or with him in his briefcase."

"Can we keep this to look it over later?" Turner asked.

"Certainly."

"Did the judge have any problems at home that you know about?" Turner asked.

"Certainly not. Judge Meade was very proud of his children. They were very successful at everything they did. He would tell us about their band concerts, their debate contests, their tennis matches, their track meets. He often took time off over the years to attend his children's events."

"How did he get along with the people he worked with?" Turner asked.

"Let me give you just one example of how wonderful he was. The judge kept a whole list of everybody's birthdays. He took up a collection once a year from everyone, so we'd all feel like we contributed, but he'd be the one to go out and buy the cake and get each of us a thoughtful little gift on our birthdays."

All the employees got along. Everything was wonderful.

They got this same refrain from the next six people they talked to. On the night of the murder, all were safely tucked in nearby suburbs celebrating with lots of corroborating witnesses.

The seventh was a tall, thin man, who walked ramrod straight. He wore highly polished black wing-tip shoes and a double-breasted, pure wool, gray plaid suit by Joseph Abboud. The oddest thing was a pince-nez dangling from a chain attached to a watch pocket in the man's vest. His name was Francis Barlow. He was in his late twenties or early thirties. He wore his hair slicked back, the wet look. Turner would have bet the rent the guy was gay.

Fenwick said, "Frank . . ."

The man interrupted, "Francis, please."

Fenwick began again, "Could you tell us . . . ?"

Francis held up his hands in a stop gesture. Before he spoke, he crossed his legs carefully. He didn't deign to adjust the crease. He knew it would be exactly where it was supposed to be. "I'll begin at the beginning. I accepted a job here out of Yale Law School. I had wanted a clerkship near home in Manhattan, but this one opened up. Before I came here, I'd never lived in a state that wasn't on a large body of water."

Obviously Lake Michigan didn't count in his pantheon of large bodies of water.

"I found it amusing when I got here to discover that one couldn't see all the way across Lake Michigan." Neither of the cops returned his half-amused grin. Barlow continued, "I discovered Judge Meade to be of average intelligence. I was forced to correct his grammar and spelling countless times on his decisions."

"Did he write his own decisions?" Turner asked.

"He scribbled out something that I helped research and then made sense out of. Essentially, he did write them, but it took an enormous amount of work on my part to have them up to proper standards. He could follow a trail of reasoning and would stay with it when challenged."

"Tell us about the other people in the office."

"Ordinary. Blanche talks about nothing but her soap operas. She tapes them daily. It makes one wish the videocassette recorder had never been invented. She gives minute-by-minute accounts in the lunchroom everyday. I was forced to find a little bistro down the street to dine in so I could have peace and quiet. The deli isn't like New York, of course. No place in Chicago really is.

"The rest are drudges. I was properly polite. I contributed to the birthday fund every year. You can't imagine how undignified it is to caterwaul at some poor unfortunate on their birthday. I had to ask the judge to forgo mine. He seemed a little put out about that. I was forced to tell him I was too shy about my birthday. They do all get along in a mindless drone sort of way. I avoid associating with them, unless absolutely unavoidable."

"How did Meade get along with the other judges?"

"Well, of course, there were the celebrated disputes with Judge Malmsted. If her logic had been more rigid and her research better, she might have made more headway. A pleasant enough woman. I agreed with her on one or two issues. Not often."

"Did you agree with Judge Meade?"

"I wasn't paid to agree with Judge Meade. I was paid to research and write."

"Besides Judge Malmsted, how did he get along with the other judges?"

"I'd say, at least, friendly with everyone, except Judge Wadsworth, of course."

"What was wrong with him?"

"I heard them argue several times."

"Judge Wadsworth said they got along fine."

"Judge Wadsworth is a fine jurist, has an excellent mind, but he was extremely remiss at being able to work with some of his fellow jurists. He likes to claim he never criticizes them. That's hypocritical nonsense. He can get quite vicious. He puts on that face to the public to try and dupe the ignorant. Those of us who know better realize he's basically a blowhard. He puts on a great show of being Solomon-like, as if he were some deity speaking from on high. Someone like Judge Meade who, for all his faults, was very independent, resented it. He and Wadsworth did not get along. They had words last week before the decision on gay rights."

"Did Wadsworth disagree with the decision?"

"I wouldn't presume to know. I use that as a time reference point. I know Judge Meade returned from a meeting with Judge Wadsworth just before they announced the decision. Judge Meade seldom showed his emotions, but there was no doubt he was extremely distressed that day. He wasn't before the meeting but he was after. The cause and effect seem logical. I did not find out what the meeting was about."

"How did they get along this week?"

"This is a light work week for federal judges. I know they

met three days before New Year's. It was a session with Wadsworth, Malmsted, and Meade. I saw Judge Meade immediately after. He didn't look happy."

"Did he say why he was unhappy?"

"Not to me."

"Know anything about Judge Meade's family?"

"I try not to involve myself in the private lives of the people I work with."

"Where were you New Year's Eve?"

"I spent the bulk of the evening at a very elegant restaurant with a friend, then returned home, where I remaincd. I read a book."

"I'll bet you did," Fenwick said.

Fenwick didn't mind sharing his feelings when dealing with pompous fools. Or too many other people, for that matter.

Fenwick continued, "We'll need to know the name of the restaurant, of your friend, and his or her address, and what was the title of the book?"

"It was *The Counterfeiters* by André Gide—in the original French, of course. I can give you my friend's name. He was visiting from New York. He left this morning." Barlow produced a small pad of paper from the interior of his suit jacket, and a silver fountain pen from the same spot. He jotted down the information they wanted on his friend, the name of the restaurant, and the hotel.

He left.

Fenwick said, "I always find that you're-a-hick-from-the-Midwest attitude so charming."

"I don't know about you," Turner said, "but I was up at four feeding the chickens and plowing the back forty, got the cows milked and the hogs slopped before breakfast."

Fenwick said, "I have hog slop envy." When he finished laughing uproariously at his own comment, he said, "Let's arrest him for the murder just for the hell of it. I bet we could get everybody who knows him to testify against him."

"All the other folks in the office said everybody got along. I bet our Francis is a big snob with them. My guess is that he goes out of his way to be correctly polite. They probably laugh at him behind his back. If he gets his work done, they probably don't complain a lot."

"Maybe if he's doing research all day, they don't see him very often."

"If they're lucky. I did like the bit about Wadsworth and Meade."

"Can't wait to hear Wadsworth's version."

They spoke with the last two employees who reverted to Blanche's version of life in Judge Meade's office. They interviewed the other judges. All confirmed Malmsted's and Meade's contretemps, but all said they didn't think she was capable of murder. All praised Wadsworth and, to a lesser extent, Meade. None claimed to have had any problems with the dead judge. None knew about arguments between Wadsworth and Meade. At eleven, Turner and Fenwick met with Judge Wadsworth.

"How did everything go?" the judge asked.

"We found out a couple things," Fenwick said. "One, you lied to us about how well everybody got along." Fenwick often confronted prominent witnesses as if he was Mayor Daley's favorite nephew and need never fear political reprisal. A federal judge couldn't specifically get you in trouble, but phone calls could be made and friends could be contacted. At the least, your ass could get chewed out or your career could get sidetracked. These possibilities seldom had much effect on Fenwick. Often, Turner tried to gently deflect Fenwick's bullish impetuosity but this worked only some of the time. In this case, it was a murder investigation and Paul wasn't in much of a mood to cater to a bunch of prima donnas.

Fenwick continued, "We've got friction between Malmsted and Meade. We also heard that you and Judge Meade often had words and did so not more than a week ago."

Wadsworth smiled benignly. "If Judge Meade and Judge Malmsted did not get along it was their business. Rulings are often the result of discussion and compromise. Sometimes that takes time. I don't call 'discussion' and 'compromise' difficulties between judges. As for me, I get along with all the people who work here. I got along with Judge Meade in the same professional manner. Everything was fine here."

"Meaning our source lied?"

"Disgruntled employees are everywhere. Only one out of how many had negative things to say?"

"All the judges were perfect? Nobody ever made a mistake?"

"We're all fallible."

"But you believe in covering up all the problems?"

"Not that I'm saying there is any, but is there a point to airing dirty linen in public?"

Fenwick growled. It didn't make much difference who was handing him a load of crap. He said, "That's a crock of shit, your honor. I hope you're not covering up information that would help us solve this case. If you have something to do with it, we'll bust your ass."

"This interview is over, gentlemen."

"Not in a homicide investigation it isn't," Fenwick said.

"I've given you all the information I can. A continuation of this interview would be fruitless."

Turner got Fenwick out of the Judge's chambers before his partner could really explode.

Fenwick's comments in the elevator down began with, "Numb-nuts, asshole, triple-fuck."

The highest rating anyone could get in Fenwick's system was "triple-fuck." Usually he reserved this sacred category for inept Bears quarterbacks when they threw game-losing interceptions, or Cubs pitchers who walked in winning runs.

The elevator was crowded, but this didn't inhibit Fenwick's rhetorical flow. An older woman with her glasses dangling from a chain around her neck turned to him at one point and said, "Young man, you may be frustrated, but you need to learn some manners. You may not speak that way when you are in my presence."

Fenwick gaped at her.

When the elevator doors swung open at the ground floor and they all exited, Turner said, "First time I've known you to be speechless in a while."

"Get me out of here before I rip the building down."

"Before we leave, let's see if that security guard who Carl Schurz mentioned is here."

They met Leo Kramer in Janice Caldwell's office. Leo's belly bulged against the heavy sweater he wore over a flannel shirt. His gray pants had gone shiny at the knees and over the butt and he wore the kind of heavy snow boots that your mother used to make you wear when you were a kid. A snake of hair crawled around his mouth in what Turner thought was the ugliest goatee he had ever seen.

Janice left them alone.

Leo licked his lips as he eyed the two detectives warily. His sparse white hair was cut short.

"What's up?" he asked.

"Heard you had a visitor New Year's Eve," Fenwick said.

"Nope. Can't say that I did. Very quiet New Year's Eve."

"None of the judges or employees came in?"

"Judge Meade signed in about eight and left a short while later."

"You didn't find that odd? He was supposed to be on his way to Canada."

"Judge Meade never did get in the habit of checking his schedule with me. Don't know why not. What is this about?"

"Guy named Carl Schurz says you and he had a little meeting here that night."

"Who?"

"You heard me," Fenwick said.

"I don't know any Carl Schurz."

"Some young man was here that night."

"Nope. Check the sign-out lists."

"How about if we check the security cameras?"

"Go ahead. I had no visitors."

Leo stuck with his denial through the rest of their questioning. When he was gone they talked with Janice Caldwell.

Fenwick said, "He claims there wasn't anybody here but himself."

"I looked through the tapes. Nobody showed up but those who signed in. There was only Judge Meade who did talk with someone in the lobby, but the camera didn't get a good shot of whoever it was. His back was to the camera. The second person did not go as far as the security checkpoint, and did not go upstairs." She gave them a complete set of tapes.

"So that part of what Schurz told us is true," Fenwick said.

"He could have seen the conversation from outside," Caldwell said.

Turner asked, "Is there any way Leo could have let someone in without it being recorded on the security cameras? If he's having meetings with young men and he's married, he wouldn't want it known. He'd want to circumvent the system."

"You're not supposed to be able to get around it. I'll have to do some investigating."

13

Turner and Fenwick stopped at Aunt Millie's for lunch. Three beat cops from the First District were singing bawdy songs in the front booth.

"You could join them," Turner said. "Maybe form a singing group."

"Let's just eat and get out."

As Fenwick wrapped his paw around a tuna melt, which he claimed was healthy and noncaloric because it was seafood, he said, "Maybe Schurz was following Meade around."

"Schurz is at the top of my suspect list along with Judge Wadsworth."

"And Francis Barlow."

"Frank the snob. We should invite him to eat here."

"Aunt Millie would ban us from the place permanently."

"And that's bad?"

After lunch they drove north, through the numbing cold. "Supposed to get up to zero today," Fenwick said. "Don't think it's going to happen."

"It's called winter, Buck. It's supposed to get cold."

At Judge Meade's home, they found friends of the deceased gathered. Turner and Fenwick took some time to question each of them briefly. None claimed to have seen the judge on the night in question. They all claimed that recently he was very happy. None of them knew of any problems.

After they finished talking to Meade's friends, Mrs. Meade led them to the judge's den. She left them alone to inspect the room. The den was much like the judge's chambers at the Kennedy Federal Building. Lots of wood, stained a bit darker here, bookcases filled with rows of similarly bound books.

"He ever read anything for pleasure?" Turner asked.

They found only nonfiction. In the middle drawer of the desk they found a calendar. They studied it carefully.

When they finished, Fenwick said, "Met with Wadsworth when Barlow said he did."

"Calendar says he was going to Canada for the conference," Turner said. "He was supposed to deliver a paper on international law. So, it was a spontaneous change of mind?"

"Or he is very devious."

"He came back to go to a gay bar? A severely closeted man can go out of his way to do all kinds of things, but a totally bogus trip? Not if he was supposed to deliver a lecture. On bogus trips you don't make commitments that have to be fulfilled."

"Maybe he had a second airline ticket for the next day. If he flew on New Year's Day, he still would have been on time for his talk today."

"We haven't found any such thing."

"Or his luggage."

"That is kind of goofy. Maybe he checked his luggage, and, in between luggage check-in and boarding the plane, something stopped him."

The desk and the rest of the room revealed nothing of interest.

They met Meade's son and daughter in the living room where they had spoken to Mrs. Meade the day before.

Pam Meade was in her middle to late twenties and Mike Meade, a few years younger. Pam had long flowing golden hair, while Mike's blond mane was pulled into a small pony tail. Both were slender and looked well muscled. Pam wore faded blue jeans and a hand-knit horizon sweater. Mike wore a slightly oversized bombay stripe shirt with a white T-shirt underneath. He wore black polar fleece pants.

Before they could begin questioning, Pam spoke. "Why hasn't my father's killer been found?"

For the next several minutes, she gave an extremely good rendition of the aggrieved relative giving the cops hell. Turner and Fenwick had heard the drill numerous times. She would stop eventually, and they would ask their questions.

Pam's mother sat on one side of her and her brother on the other. In the middle of her tirade, she began to cry. Mrs. Meade put her arm around her daughter, and Mike patted her arm.

When equilibrium returned, Mike said, "What can we do to help?" This was said with manly assurance, mixed with an awkward quaver he couldn't completely conceal—I'm the surviving male adult here—with tears lurking just underneath.

"We know this is a difficult time, but we need to ask a few questions," Turner said.

Mike nodded.

"Do you know if your father had any enemies?" Turner asked.

"Not that I know of," Mike said.

Pam said, "Well, all those left-wing groups were mad at him at one time or another. They were always denouncing him. One of the groups even demonstrated in front of the house once."

"Which group was that?"

"I don't remember. The police were here. They'd have a record. Some group that thought they knew best."

"You agreed with your father's politics?" Turner asked.

"When we were kids we fought some," Pam said. "But over the years, I learned he was doing his best in difficult situations and that there were seldom clear-cut answers to many questions. Sometimes he had to make difficult choices. He thought deeply, read a lot, put a lot of himself into his decisions."

"How about you, Mike?" Fenwick asked.

"I loved my dad. We didn't discuss politics a lot."

"Where were you both on New Year's Eve?" Turner asked.

"I had volunteered to go back to school for this week," Mike said. "I was in Bloomington-Normal. I'm a fifth-year senior at Illinois State University. I'm involved in a major project this summer for my degree and had to do a lot of the preplanning. It involves a lot of youngsters at a camp in Vermont. I was staying at a friend's house off campus."

"I was in California at a Young Republican woman's symposium," Pam said.

Turner wrote down the basic information and would check it out later.

In the car Fenwick said, "Kids seemed okay. Cried at the right moments. Properly indignant."

"Wouldn't want them to be improperly indignant."

When they walked into Au Naturel, all the lights were on. Two fully clothed young men were hard at work. One pushed an industrial-strength floor waxer and buffer. The other was busy dusting and polishing. They found Dana Sickles in her office.

She gave them a sour look. "Business was shit last night. Thank you very much."

"Just trying to help out," Fenwick said.

"What do you want?"

"We have another confirmation that the judge was in the bar last night."

"I know I'm supposed to care about this."

"Just following where the facts lead," Fenwick said.

Turner said, "Our source says the judge was talking to one of the dancers about nine o'clock."

"Here?"

"No. In the Loop."

"You're source really gets around. He following the judge?"

"We don't think so."

"We need you to tell us if you recognize the guy. We're looking for somebody with huge pecs, reddish-blond hair, flat stomach, and wearing a red thong."

She burst out laughing.

"I missed the funny part," Fenwick said.

"That describes half the boys. In the light around here the blonds can go from dark to light. Red thong? They often trade outfits. Something looks hot on one, or somebody makes a lot of money wearing a certain thing, they all want to wear it. Your description isn't going to get you anywhere."

"We haven't talked to all the guys who work here yet," Turner said, "and we need to talk to all the others again."

"Why don't you just bring your source down here and have him identify the suspect?"

Turner looked sheepish. "We're having trouble locating our source. He seems to have disappeared."

"Are you guys serious?"

"Most of the time," Fenwick said.

"We need the guys here," Turner said. "If you could have them here by four, we could be done by the time you wanted to open."

"The implication being that if I don't get them here then I don't open?"

"We know you want to help the police," Fenwick said. "We know good Republicans are supposed to be on the side of the upholders of the law."

"They let cops be sarcastic with the public?" she asked.

"Only me. I have a special permit."

She agreed to do what she could to get all the dancing boys assembled by four.

Turner and Fenwick walked down the street to the used bookstore. A huge Going-Out-of-Business sign hung in the front window. Inside was a mass of confusion. About half the books were in boxes while the other half were still on the shelves. Mounds of maps and charts were strewn on the front counter. A large, gray, long-haired cat lay curled in the open cash-register drawer.

They found a stooped man in his late seventies in the back feeding a pot-bellied pig. Turner noticed the place had a distinct barnyard odor. If the place could remain open a little longer, he thought he would recommend it to Francis Barlow.

The man smiled at them from under bushy eyebrows. He wore a tattered cardigan sweater over faded blue jeans.

Turner consulted his notes. "Mr. Hays?"

"Yes, gentleman. Everything is half price. I can help you with what is on the shelves, but you'll have to look through the boxes yourselves."

Turner showed him his identification.

Hays brushed the dirt off his hands. "Don't know much. You guys must be really reaching for something. Course, big case like this, must be lots of pressure. Not as much as that nonsense in Los Angeles. Course, that means you won't get as famous."

"What do you know, Mr. Hays?"

"They must of told you it wasn't much. All I know is I was working here until after three last night. They're foreclosing in days. Some people's retirement dreams come true. Mine didn't. Luckily I didn't let myself go broke with this operation. Got a nice little place in Texas where I can do some fishing and not have to live through another of these hellish winters."

"The report said you heard something."

"Little before two. I was listening to the New Year's Eve Midnight Special on WFMT. They'd just got done with the live portion, that's how I remember the time. I was in back there. He pointed to what resembled an office—desks, calculator, ledger books. "Trying to squeeze a dime or two more out of the business." He shook his head. "Like I said, it was just after two. Heard this car. Didn't think much of it. It's an alley you know, supposed to be cars. Heard this kind of crush or crunch. Loud, you know. Thought it was those damn kids setting off firecrackers, or maybe shooting guns. Hell of a way to celebrate a New Year, making noise. I always prefer quiet celebrations with friends."

"You didn't investigate?"

"No. It was loud, but it was just the one."

"Could have been a gun shot?"

"Maybe. The young cops that were here earlier asked me for 'anything.' That was as much 'anything' as I could come up with."

They gave him their number and returned to Area Ten Headquarters.

The woman at the downstairs desk greeted them with, "Commander wants to see you."

"What'd you guys do this time?" a uniform asked.

"Arrested the mayor," Fenwick said.

Upstairs they found the acting commander. He invited them into his office. He sat behind a cluttered desk. Turner and Fenwick rested in metal chairs in front of him.

"Got a call about you both," Molton said.

"Who wants to give us a medal now?" Fenwick said.

"Judge Wadsworth called to complain."

Fenwick said, "Golly shucks, we've been bad. Screw that stupid shit."

Molton said, "What have you got so far?"

They told him.

When they finished he said, "You've been doing fine. I can't think of anything else you should have done or could be doing. Forget about the judge. I only told you because it adds a dimension to the case, and you need to know everything. He didn't like your way of questioning him. I may not like it either, but calling me sure as hell made me suspicious."

"He claims he was having a quiet evening at home," Turner said.

"Doesn't anybody go out on New Year's any more?" Molton said. "Confirm everybody's whereabouts. Copies of all of Meade's decisions are here, and so are most of the reports from the medical examiner."

The first thing they checked was the ME's reports. They flipped through their copies and traded bits of information as they read.

"Blood on the pavement was definitely his," Turner said.

"No drugs, moderate amount of alcohol, was not drunk," Fenwick added.

"Didn't recover the bullet. No definite type on the gun. Big. Killed him instantly."

They read for ten more minutes.

"Anything in this we didn't know already?" Turner asked.

"Not much. Having a hard time telling the time of death because the body was frozen. Took more time to do the autopsy because they had to thaw the body. Weird."

"If the old man is right, we've got a time of death around two."

"If what he heard was really the shot that killed him, and we don't have a mess in the alley, it means the killer has a very messy car."

"Judge Meade had been drinking."

Fenwick said, "Presumably not drinking at home."

"Unless his wife is lying."

"I think she was telling the truth. Most probably, he was out somewhere. No friends have come forward to say he was with them. If they were telling the truth, then he was drinking in a public place, which we have concluded was Au Naturel."

"Could have been another bar."

"I'm not going to send a cop to every bar in the city."

"Who's the resident expert on the nut groups in the city? Those abortion people are crazy enough to kill. We've got to check them out." Turner spent several minutes calling bureaucrats at police headquarters before he got Melissa Baker, detective in charge of loonies traveling to the city.

"You the terrorism squad?" Turner asked.

"No, just a cop like you trying to make a living. What can I do for you?"

Turner explained about needing to know about possible attacks on federal judges.

Baker answered promptly. "At this time, none of the known troublemakers from any anti-abortion or other terrorist group is in town."

"You know this off the top of your head?"

"That's what they pay me to know. What I, of course, can't tell you is if there are any unknown crazed killers in town. You can always get some loony in some fringe group trying to be a hero. I can tell you we haven't gotten one call from any group claiming to have offed the judge. I'll do some checking, but I think this is all I'll be able to get for you in the way of information. This case doesn't feel political to me."

Turner thanked her, hung up, and filled Fenwick in.

Wilson and Roosevelt walked in and came over.

"No luck on Carl Schurz," Wilson said. "Not easy to find a homeless drifter. Lot of these runaway kids show up at the bus station. Got a mini-lead. An old guy named Roman Ayres hangs out there. In his seventies."

"You have a source who's a child molester?" Fenwick asked.

"Have all your sources been saints?"

"He ever been busted for trying to have sex with the kids?" Fenwick asked.

"No, but he's our source," Wilson said. "One of the cops that works that beat knows him. Supposedly this guy doesn't want sex with the kids. None of the teens he's worked with have ever complained. Very few of the boys he's helped have gotten in trouble with the police."

"Sort of a one-man halfway house," Roosevelt said.

Wilson continued, "He has a decent reputation with the cop we talked to. He said the guy's story is that his parents threw him out of his house back in the thirties. He had no place to go then. Now that he's retired, he wants to help these kids who are just off the bus, like he was. We couldn't get a lead from any of Schurz's peers. We were lucky to find this guy."

Turner wrote down the name and address. "We've got to interview the people at the bar again." Turner explained what they'd learned that day.

Judy Wilson said, "Any studly black guys are mine."

"You're married," Roosevelt said.

"I didn't say I wanted to mate with them, but I could dance with them."

Turner called Ian and asked, "You ever heard of a Roman Ayres? Supposedly, he works with the kids just off the bus, runaways. Gay kids who've been thrown out of their homes."

"I heard of him, but I never met him. We wanted to do an article on him. He wants no credit, notoriety, or thanks. Usually that means he's diddling the kids, but my sources say he's a genuinely kind man who just wants to help quietly. He connected to this?"

"Maybe." He told them what Roosevelt and Wilson had.

The detectives had an hour before they were due back at the bar. Turner and Fenwick spent the time catching up on paperwork. Wilson began thumbing through the judge's decisions. She made notes of groups she thought might have been angered by a decision. Roosevelt went through the mountain of press clippings one of the researchers had assembled. Most were from the two local newspapers, the *Tribune* and the *Sun-Times,* but a few were from the *New York Times.* He also made notes summarizing possible groups that the judge might have made angry and wrote down the names of anyone from a group that made statements after the rulings.

They assigned beat cops to meet with leaders of each of the groups for preliminary interviews. Turner agreed with Baker that this was not a political murder, and talking to these people was probably useless, but it had to be done. At this time in the investigation they had at least thirty cops, either full or part time, at their disposal. If somebody got lucky and broke the case, they could get themselves on all kinds of newscasts.

Turner and Fenwick left half an hour early for the bar. They drove to the address they had for Roman Ayres. He lived on Racine Avenue just north of Diversey. His apartment was on the top floor of a three-flat.

Ayres moved, spoke, and acted with quiet dignity. His face

was pock-marked and wrinkled. His white hair was cut short. Tufts of hair stuck out of both ears. The fabric on his cloth-covered couch and chair was threadbare. He had a twelve-inch-screen television. The apartment was humid to the point of uncomfortableness and the walls were barren.

After identification and introduction, Turner explained about Carl Schurz.

When he finished Ayres said, "You're the gay cop, aren't you?"

"Yes," Turner said.

"I could tell. I can always tell. Carl told me about you. You care about this kid?"

"I don't want him to be hurt."

"I don't have to be careful about my emotions with them. I can give them my heart. Doesn't matter if they break it or disappoint me. I'm old."

"When did you see Carl?" Turner asked.

"He came to see me last night. I tell them they can come anytime they want. When people are in need, they don't always have a good sense of time. He talked about you a lot, Detective Turner."

"I didn't lead him on."

"Carl laughed about that. He thought you might fall off the end of the desk." Ayres frowned. "He talked a great deal about you holding him."

Turner began a protest.

"I believe you didn't want to lead him on. He just talked about you holding him. Your confidence and self-assurance. Your good looks and how sexually attracted he was to you."

"Look, Mr. Ayres . . ."

"I'm not saying this to embarrass you. I'm just reporting. He said he wanted to be like you when he grew up."

Turner sat back for a moment. "I only talked to him for that short time."

"He was in desperate need. All these runaways are. They can

quickly form very powerful attachments. You'd be surprised how many of these kids are looking for an older man. You could probably get all Freudian and talk about looking for love and approval from their fathers. Maybe that would be on target. At any rate, you did nothing wrong, I'm sure. Not from what Carl said. I know Carl and how he can be—how they can all be."

"I wish I could help him."

"Don't we all desperately want the world to come out right—for it to be perfect in ways it can never possibly be? You did your best. How can I help you?"

"Do you know where he went?"

"Not specifically. He didn't stay here the night. I can give you a couple places to check. I know the boys hang out several places. One of the most common is on Lower Wacker Drive. Lot of drugs down there."

"In this cold?"

"Drugs know no season. Try there. He probably won't be there, but the local drug pusher will know him. Wouldn't your beat cops be able to help with that? The cross street aboveground is Monroe. On Lower Wacker there's a narrow recess between buildings that turns into a walkway which meanders deep beneath the streets. Follow it back and it opens up to a larger space. If the pusher gives you trouble, well, I'm sure you have ways to get him to be cooperative. You may have to use them. Now, in this neighborhood, I'd try on Broadway north of Belmont. There's a halfway house for runaway teens which he stayed at for a while."

"He into drugs?"

"He isn't an addict. I have some hopes that he'll escape that. I always have hopes, though. If he's lucky, he isn't hooked. Those are the two most likely places in this weather."

In the car Turner said, "I feel so sorry for that kid. I hope we find him. I don't know if I can help him, but maybe at least we can find him a warm place for a few days."

"Lots of people have tried to help him," Fenwick said. "Some people who need help don't know what they want. Some won't take the help. You're not a social worker."

"I know. I just . . ." Turner stared out at the cold while Fenwick drove.

14

Just after four o'clock, Turner and Fenwick met Roosevelt and Wilson at Au Naturel. The interior of the bar was filled with what must have been the largest single gathering of hot male flesh since William Higgins' classic porn video *Class Reunion.*

"That one's mine," Wilson said. She nodded toward a well-muscled black man.

Roosevelt said, "You have excellent taste."

After an hour and a half of interrogating, however, they got absolutely nothing for their trouble.

Finally the detectives got the entire group together. Dana Sickles stood next to the detectives.

"Who's not here?" Fenwick asked.

Several guys raised their hands.

Sickles said, "I kept a list from yesterday and today. Between them you got everybody but two. I haven't been able to get hold of them, which is not that uncommon."

"Who were they?"

She consulted the list. "Jim Barnes and Lance Thrust."

The four cops stared at her.

"Lance Thrust is his real name?" Turner asked.

"We pay in cash."

Fenwick said, "You have to have an address to send W2s, a real name and a social security number."

Sickles told them to wait. She returned from her office in a few moments. She handed them the two applications.

Barnes lived at an address in Wicker Park. Lance Thrust listed his home as six twenty-three School Street.

The bar owner said, "I never had to mail him anything. Generally, W2s are handed to them. Those who are around. Some move and never get them. I try my best. This is a transitory profession. Taxes are their problem."

"Tell me about Barnes and Thrust," Turner said.

"Sounds like a pornographic law firm," Fenwick said.

Sickles said, "Barnes claimed he was straight, but he said he wanted to give dancing a try. He heard the money was good, and he thought it might be fun. Been working here for about a month. Thrust has been here since last January. Longer than most of them. Did his job. Neither guy caused any trouble. Got here on time. Got lots of compliments from the customers."

"Either one a reddish blond?"

"Both are light blond." She pointed at the red-and green-track lights above the dancing platform. "We put those in for the season. Could easily dim or enhance skin, hair, eye color. You saw the lights in the dressing room."

Turner asked the assembled dancers if any of them were friends with Barnes or Thrust. Most shrugged. One or two looked uncomfortable.

"Nobody dances and nobody works until we get some information about them," Fenwick said.

Sickles began a protest.

Fenwick said, "I'm tired of this crap. If we don't get information, we'll find a way to shut you down." He glared at her and then at the employees.

None of them moved.

Dana said, "Look, why don't you step down to the corner for a cup of coffee. Let me talk to them. You're not going to get anywhere by bullying them."

"I want answers," Fenwick said.

"Why don't I just call my lawyer and we'll all get nowhere together? My lawyer will be happy to slow you down as much as he can."

"Do you really think he can stop us if we're determined?"

"Going to run an inspection? Get ten or fifteen cops in here just to check my license?"

"We need to get some questions answered," Turner said. "We can do it simply and relatively painlessly, or we can go through a big hassle and do it the hard way."

"I suppose you could shut me down, or ruin the place for good, if it hasn't been already." She sighed. "Give me a chance."

"We'll give you time to talk to them," Turner said.

The cops left. Wilson and Roosevelt drove off to pursue one of their own cases. After fifteen minutes in the coffee shop, Fenwick began to get restless. After half an hour, he was drawing faces in the ice on the inside of the huge picture windows.

Thirty-five minutes later, they saw Dana Sickles emerge from her bar. A herd of bundled-up male flesh trailed after her. They quickly scattered. Dana entered the coffee shop alone.

She ordered a cup of coffee and joined them. "Thank you for leaving."

"Seemed reasonable," Turner said. "As long as we get some information."

"I've got a couple things for you. If you want to talk to the guys who gave me the information, fine. I got them to agree to that."

Fenwick grumbled, "How lucky for us."

"Barnes has moved recently. He's living in a building on the southeast corner of Belmont and Lake Shore Drive."

"He can afford that?"

"The guys think he has a sugar daddy."

"I thought he was straight," Turner said.

"Are any of these guys really straight? Maybe so, but if you offer a guy enough money, straight or gay, who knows?"

"Name of the guy?" Fenwick asked.

"Can you be a bit less aggressive? I've got the drill down."

She pointed at Turner first, then Fenwick. "You're 'good cop' and he's 'bad cop.' Don't you get tired of it?"

Fenwick said, "Sometimes we switch."

"He's in apartment seventeen-oh-three."

"How about Mr. Thrust?"

"Couldn't get a real name out of them. One of the dancers said he went back to Thrust's apartment with him once to have sex. This was Christmas Eve and Thrust was pretty drunk. None of the other guys said they ever went home with him. It was the first apartment building west of the El tracks on Loyola Avenue. North side of the street. He didn't remember the address."

"Name of your source," Fenwick said.

"You can beat it out of me if you want, copper." She gave them the names and left.

Turner and Fenwick drove to Belmont and Sheridan. The door to 1703 was opened by a man who Turner thought might be in his late thirties. He wore black jeans and a white banded collar shirt. He frowned at them uncertainly.

"How did you get past the doorman?"

They showed him their identification.

"May we come in, Mr. Rice?" They'd gotten his name from the doorman.

"Certainly."

As Rice closed the door, another man, clad only in boxer shorts, entered the room. He was in his late teens or early twenties with broad shoulders and a flat stomach.

"This the other two guys?" the boxer shorts man said.

Rice caught sight of him. "This is the police."

"Oh." The kid stood uncertainly.

"We'd like to talk to both of you," Turner said.

The kid sat down on a couch. Rice remained standing. "We're investigating the murder of Judge Meade," Turner said.

"Why come here?" Rice asked.

"We need to ask a few questions," Turner said. He focused on the younger man. "You're James Barnes?"

"Yeah."

"You were at Au Naturel on New Year's Eve?"

He nodded.

"How about you, Mr. Rice?"

"I was home reading a book."

"A dancer with blond hair was seen talking to Judge Meade that night."

"Wasn't me," the kid said. "I don't know any Judge Meade. Who is he?" His voice was deep and sensuous. Turner wished he'd put on more clothes.

"He was murdered."

"Oh, I think I heard about that. Dana's been calling around for everybody. Somebody told me, but I was planning to quit so I ignored it."

Fenwick looked at Rice then back to Barnes, "Did you find a better job?"

Rice and Barnes kept silent.

Turner showed Barnes the picture of the judge. "You remember if he gave you money that night?"

"Hundreds of guys gave me money that night. I couldn't tell you one from another."

Neither one admitted to anything more. Turner and Fenwick left. Just coming off the elevator as the detectives were entering were two men dressed in black leather from boots to cap. Each carried a large gym bag.

As the doors to the elevator closed Turner said, "Mr. Barnes seems to have gotten himself a fan club."

Fenwick said, "The authors in the world would be pleased at the amount of reading occurring in Chicago on New Year's Eve."

"We're close to the address on Belmont that Roman Ayres gave us for Carl Schurz."

They stopped at the halfway house. The social worker in

charge said, "I saw him late yesterday. He didn't look good. Is he in trouble?"

"We just need to talk to him. He's a witness in a case."

"That kid is very fragile. It wouldn't take much to put him over the edge."

No one else at the halfway house had seen or admitted to seeing Carl.

In the car Fenwick said, "It's only a block or so, let's check on Mr. Thrust on School Street." Their hunt for 623 was brief. School Street stopped at Clark and became Aldyne. There was no 623. They drove to Rogers Park to investigate the building they'd been given as a place one of the dancers had met with Thrust for sex.

The directry at the apartment house did not list any Thrusts or Lances. Fenwick rang the bell for the manager. A portly gentleman answered. They identified themselves as police officers. He let them into his apartment. He had a pit-bull terrier and about a million plants. The dog growled and snarled even after he was placed behind a closed door.

"Betsy doesn't like strangers," he said.

They asked about Lance Thrust.

"No one by that name lives here. Is this a joke?"

Turner remembered that Lance had started work at Au Naturel in January. "Any tenants come to live here in the past year?" Turner asked. "Especially last January?"

"I've had six new tenants. I'll get you their names." He produced a ledger book. He showed them the names.

"No Lance, no Thrust," Fenwick said.

Turner didn't recognize any of the names.

"Any of them young men, probably good looking, in good shape, might belong to a gym?"

"Got to be Malcolm," the manager said instantly. "Three of the others are women. Two are older guys who are definitely not in shape."

"Tell us about Malcolm," Turner urged.

"Not much to tell. He's very quiet. Always pays his rent on

time. Odd though, he always pays in cash. Most folks write checks. I have to give him a receipt."

"Anybody else fitting that description move in last year?" Turner asked.

"No. Malcolm's a looker. One of a kind. Don't get them that hot around here unless they're from the university. They usually can't afford this place and we don't let them put ten in an apartment. We have strict limits."

"He wasn't going to school?"

"Never saw him with any books."

"Can we see his apartment?"

"What's he done?"

"We're investigating a murder."

"He kill somebody?"

"We just need to talk to him."

"I guess I could let you in. That's not violating his rights, is it?"

"Not if you let us in."

"Oh."

They followed him into the hall. Behind them, the lobby door swung open. Turner looked back. The evening gloom showed a blond-haired male. Mike Meade stood in the doorway.

15

Meade gasped, turned, and ran. His gym bag banged against a plastic reindeer on the lawn as he bolted across it. The reindeer plopped over and the right antler shattered on a patch of ice. Meade flung the gym bag away. He ran toward the El station. Turner leapt over the reindeer while Fenwick lumbered around it.

Fenwick quickly fell farther behind. It would be a long time before he won a race with an athletic twenty-two year old. Turner wouldn't have caught him either, except the kid's winter jacket got entangled in the door handle of the El station. Meade yanked at it for a few seconds, and then thrust himself out of the coat. By then Turner had him by the scruff of the neck.

The kid squirmed and punched for a few seconds. He hit Turner in the middle of his winter coat but multiple layers of heavy clothes prevented the blow from having much effect.

Puffing spasmodically, Fenwick arrived. He grabbed the kid's wrists.

Meade yelled, "Help, robbery, I'm being mugged!" while continuing to squirm.

"Hold still, you little shit!" Fenwick barked.

A small crowd began to gather. Turner held up his identification.

With a sudden thrust, Fenwick knocked the kid to the

ground, sat on his butt, whipped the kid's left arm back, applied the handcuff, and then snatched the other wrist.

"That hurts!" the kid yelled. Turner saw tears start down his cheeks.

"It's supposed to," Fenwick said.

They yanked him to his feet. Turner searched him, but found no weapons.

Meade was silent as they brought him back to the apartment house, picked up his gym bag, and proceeded inside.

"We need to see your apartment," Fenwick said.

"I don't live here."

Turner banged on the manager's door. It burst open as if the occupant were eagerly listening with his ear to the other side.

Fenwick pointed at Mike Meade. "He claims he doesn't live here. You were going to show us an apartment?"

"Of course he lives here, and he pays his rent on time. Malcolm what's wrong?"

Meade hung his head.

"He couldn't identify himself earlier," Fenwick said, "but now he knows who he is, probably kind of a Generation X, dark-night-of-the-soul type of thing."

"Oh," the manager said.

To Mike Meade, Turner said, "We can talk to you here, down at the station, or up in your apartment."

"In the apartment," he muttered.

The manager looked disappointed that he wouldn't be able to be part of, or at least witness to, more of a show. "Any help you need," he called after them.

Fenwick stood near the entrance with Meade while Turner inspected the apartment. The heat was on and the atmosphere crackled with dry electricity. The apartment had one main room with space slightly larger than an alcove for the kitchen. Small refrigerator, two burner stove, tiny sink, even tinier table on which they piled their coats. In the living room a fold-out couch was the only furniture. It stood next to a short, squat radiator painted white. The closet was part of the hallway leading to the bathroom. The storage space for clothes consisted of three narrow drawers. One had underwear, the other neatly rolled-up socks, the third two sweaters and two pairs of jeans. Four neatly ironed shirts hung on a rack attached to the top of the door.

The bathroom gleamed. In the cabinet were a razor, shaving cream, toothpaste, and a toothbrush. In the narrow space a tall thin radiator provided heat.

They left the cuffs on the kid and put him on the couch. Since he'd run, they'd keep him in restraints.

Fenwick sat in the chair. Turner leaned against the doorway leading to the closet.

"What's going on?" Turner asked. "You're Malcolm. The manager knows you as the one living here, and you're Lance Thrust the dancer at Au Naturel. Why does Mike Meade go through all this elaborate deception?"

"Why the hell do you think?"

"Why don't you tell me?" Turner said.

"Have I done something illegal?"

"Your father has been murdered. His son is leading a double or triple life. You ran from the cops. I think that gives us a wide latitude in finding out what you've been up to."

Mike Meade stood up. Fenwick planted himself in front of the exit.

"I'm not going to run," Mike said. He nodded over his shoulder at his still cuffed hands. "Can't you take these off?"

"No," Fenwick stated.

Mike Meade wore white athletic shoes, faded blue jeans, a hand-woven Guatemalan shirt, and a sheepskin vest. Turner did not remember him as one of the dancers from New Year's Eve.

Meade walked to the one window looking out on Loyola Avenue. He stretched his arms and shoulders as much as he could against the cuffs, and leaned his forehead on the glass and spoke to the street below. He muttered, "Everything is so fucked up."

He was silent for a few moments, then turned and leaned his shoulders against the window and continued, "I haven't been in school for more than a year. I didn't tell my parents I quit. I had a full academic scholarship to the university. I just dropped out. Part of the reason was that I got sick and tired of my gay friends asking me how my dad could support legislation that denied gay people their rights. When I told them he didn't know I was gay, some would be sympathetic, but lots of them thought I should confront him. That I owed it to the gay community, whatever the hell that is. One of my friends wanted to out me, sort of the reverse of the way that straight colonel did with his gay son. How that would get my father to support legislation favorable to gays, nobody ever said. Look at Phyllis Schlafly and her kid. He's gay, but she's still against gay rights."

"You never told your dad you were gay?" Turner asked.

"I hadn't."

"What happened?"

"I left school a year ago Christmas. I needed money. Mom and dad gave me an allowance, but it wasn't nearly enough for me to pay expenses on my own. I kept an address off campus. My parents gave me enough so that I could just pay the rent on that one. They sent everything to that address. I couldn't get any kind of job in Bloomington. I didn't know what to do. What the hell was I supposed to do? I've got no skills. No degree. I used to hang out in one of the gay bars in Bloomington. Once or twice guys had offered me money to go home with them. They were old and fat so I said no. When I'd been living on beans, bread, and water for two months, I thought about selling myself. I figured if I could be more selective, maybe I could handle it. I talked to a friend I knew who was a hustler. He'd begun dancing at Au Naturel. I liked that idea even better. If I didn't want to be a call boy, I wouldn't. I'm lucky to be in decent shape. My friend brought me down there. I applied, auditioned, and got the job. I could dance and pick the guys I wanted to go home with when I wanted. I made good money. Enough to set me up here."

"You hustled," Fenwick stated.

Meade shrugged as best he could. "Sure. I found out I liked making guys feel good for a few minutes. I was good at making old guys feel loved. Is that so bad?"

"Why not just go home?" Turner asked. "Just tell them . . ."

Meade interrupted. "You're cops. You're not gay. You wouldn't understand."

"No, I meant just tell them you quit school. Thousands of kids do it every day."

"I wasn't going to live a closeted life at home. I wanted to make it on my own. I wasn't really doing that in Bloomington. Everybody talks about coming out as if it were so much safer and easier than it was twenty-five years ago and, for some people, maybe it is. For me, it wasn't. My father was a horrible tyrant."

"Did he abuse you?" Turner asked.

"Not physically. It was emotional control. I had to measure up. I had to be perfect. Being gay was not part of being perfect. I wish I wasn't gay. If someone offered me a magic wish, I'd wish I could change. I'd rather be straight. I hate being gay."

"What happened New Year's Eve?" Turner asked.

"I wasn't in Bloomington. I'd gone skiing in Aspen for three days with a wealthy client. That kept me out of the house for a good part of what was supposedly my Christmas vacation from school. I wouldn't have to be in my dad's presence. After the client was finished with me, I relaxed for a few days by myself. I flew back through St. Louis and spent a day there. I was flying back that night to go to work at the bar. I didn't want to miss my New Year's Eve shift. You can make a lot of money dancing on New Year's Eve. The weather in St. Louis was terrible. For a while I didn't think we'd be taking off but finally we did, three hours late. I didn't even think about my dad being at the airport until we were in the air. I couldn't remember when he was supposed to leave. I wasn't even sure he was leaving on the thirty-first, much less what time of day.

"I met a friend at the airport. I figured this next part out later from what my dad said. He saw me from a distance and tried to catch up. He didn't know I was going to be there. Before he could catch up, my friend and I kissed and hugged good-bye. After that, my father didn't approach me. He followed me to the El. It was crowded with the people rushing back from the airport trying to beat the jammed highways. I never saw him. I was late, and I only had my gym bag, so I went straight to the bar. I took the El back and then a cab from downtown. Traffic was still a mess so it wasn't hard for him to get a cab and follow me. I never even looked back. Who would have noticed? Nobody expects to be followed. I sure didn't."

Turner said, "Your mother and sister never mentioned anything about any fights between you and your dad."

"Why would they? They know I wouldn't kill my dad, but mentioning the fights would have made me a suspect."

"They lied to the police," Fenwick said.

"Well, golly, I'll bet they're the first ones that ever fibbed to you."

Fenwick said, "You've got a smart mouth for somebody who just ran from the police investigating a murder."

"Sorry, I'll go back to being passive and intimidated just to make you happy."

Fenwick said, "As long as you keep talking, I'm happy."

Turner said, "No one where your father worked or any of his friends said anything about fights between the two of you."

Mike Meade continued. "We might be arguing like mad before a guest came to the house, but once somebody else walked in, you'd have thought we were Ozzie and Harriet mixed with the Brady Bunch. You really think it's that odd that a family keeps its business to itself?"

"Who was the friend you were with in St. Louis?" Fenwick asked.

"Who I was with has nothing to do with the investigation."

"Not answering makes you look bad," Fenwick said.

"I don't have to tell you."

Turner asked, "At the bar that night, did you hear the announcement Billy Geary made about your dad being in the bar?"

"No. Billy made an announcement?"

"You know who he is?"

"Yeah. He's not a close friend, but I know who he is."

"Does he know who you are?"

"No. None of them did. Only one of them even knew where I lived. That was one guy I brought back here. He must have told you about this place. My moment of lust was a mistake."

"What happened between you and your dad at Au Naturel?"

"At the bar I changed and made it just in time for my first set."

"What time was this?"

"A little after ten."

"How long did you dance?"

"About fifteen minutes."

"Was it worth it?" Fenwick asked.

"What do you mean?"

"How much money did you make?"

"In fifteen minutes I had over one hundred dollars and two offers of a great deal more."

Turner looked at him. Young, blond, a few boyish freckles, broad shoulders, a narrow waist. Men would pay a great deal for what Mike Meade had.

"What happened with your dad?"

"After my fourth set, sometime after one, I saw him while I was dancing. At first I couldn't believe it. The crowd had started to thin out a little by then. He just sat in the darkest corner—the one on the other side of the pinball machines. The wildest things went through my mind. What was he doing there? Was my dad gay and this was his way of coming out to me? He'd made all those horrible rulings, and he was a closet case? I was ashamed of him more than I'd ever been. It was supremely weird being in a sexual situation with your dad sitting there. I was also curious. Maybe a little scared."

"Why?"

"He has a temper."

"Nobody we've talked to said that."

"At work he was this right-wing saint. To me, he was a terror."

"How did he treat your mother and sister?"

"He was good to them. But I was the son. I had to be the best. That night, I didn't know what to do. I was barely able to finish that set. He knew I saw him, and I couldn't stop looking at him. After I was done, I went back to the dressing room and put on my clothes and went back out front. It's up to us if we want to go out and work the crowd."

"Work the crowd?" Fenwick asked.

"When we're not dancing some of the guys go out and nuzzle up to men who gave them money, especially those who paid more than a buck or two. It wasn't really necessary that night. With all that booze and wild partying, the guys were paying well."

"You confronted your dad?"

"He was still sitting where I had seen him. I walked up to him. I'll never forget it."

He paused, wandered around the room, stared out the window, and finally sat back down on the couch. He stared down at the maroon, rose-patterned carpet. "He wouldn't look at me. The first thing he said was, 'How could you be so stupid?'

"I said, 'Dad, I'm gay.'

"He said, 'I'm not as stupid as you.'

"Partly I was kind of embarrassed, I mean your dad seeing you mostly naked being pawed by a bunch of strangers? It's like thinking about your parents having sex. I'm sure parents don't fantasize about their kids having sex. I was also pissed off. He still hadn't looked at me. Calling me stupid had been one of his manipulations when I was a kid. When I was little, he'd say, 'Do you want to be stupid all your life?' I came to hate it. When it was certain that I'd won a full academic scholarship to college, he and I had a huge fight the next time he called me stupid. I was determined that the next time he said it, I'd let him have it."

"What happened?"

"It was the night of the senior prom. He'd been leering and talking all night about the prom being a rite of teenage passage. I told him it was just a dance. He told me not to be stupid. We had a shouting match that lasted half an hour. My mother and sister had to get between us or we'd probably have hit each other."

"Does your mother or your sister know you're gay?" Turner asked.

"My sister does, Mom doesn't, although she might have guessed."

"You went to the prom?" Fenwick asked.

"You can read a few headlines about kids taking same-sex dates to the prom. It doesn't happen. Not in the real world, at least, not in my real world." He looked at the two cops. "I tried to have sex with the girl I was with. Nothing happened. I couldn't get it up. Does that shock you?"

The detectives remained silent.

"It shocked me and scared me. The week after, the guy I wished I'd had the nerve to take to the prom, turned out to be as interested in me as I was in him. That's when I admitted to myself I was gay.

"That shouting match with my dad wasn't the first, but it was the worst and the last. We avoided each other a lot after that. The summer vacation after high school, I worked as a counselor in Wyoming at a Republican Youth summer camp. Those people are real crazies. Then I went away to school but, when I came home, like for the holidays, everything was really tense. We avoided each other. I'd go out with friends, be anywhere except in his presence.

"Anyway, being called stupid sets me off, and that night at the bar, I got really angry."

"Didn't people notice your argument?" Fenwick asked.

"The noise level in the front room of the bar is usually a zillion decibels into the dangerous zone. New Year's Eve is worse. You have to shout to be heard inches away. They couldn't hear us. Most everybody looks at the stage or people they know."

"What else did you say to each other?"

"I positioned myself so he was wedged between a bar stool, the wall, and a pinball machine. He'd have to trample over me to get out. He finally glanced in my direction. I said, 'I'm not ashamed of what I do. I am not stupid. You are. You're the ignorant bigot in the family. You're the one who can't write his own decisions on the court, who has to get other people to write them. You're the one who hasn't had the brains.' He said, 'I'm not the one stupid enough to be a whore.' I said, 'What are you doing here? Do you like what you see?' For a few seconds I thought he was going to hit me. I probably deserved it. I know I felt like hitting him and he certainly deserved it. Finally, he said, 'This place disgusts me.'

"I didn't say anything for a minute, then I asked him how he knew I was there. That's when he told me about the airport. I can't believe it, a few minutes in either direction, and we'd have never seen each other. No snow in St. Louis, and he might still be alive."

"What do you mean?"

"He'd have gone on to Montreal. He'd still be alive."

"Then what happened at the bar?" Turner asked.

"He said, 'If you leave with me now, we'll save your mother a lot of grief.'

"I told him that was a crock of shit. I said that he shouldn't hide behind my mother. Then I said, 'I'm gay and proud of it.' " He swept his arm around the bar and said, 'You're proud of this? That's pathetic and stupid.'

"I lost my temper. I told him to fuck off. I told him he was a Neanderthal creep. I told him hateful things that I am never going to be able to take back."

Mike leaned forward and stared at the floor. Turner couldn't see the young man's face, but he saw tears falling onto the carpet. "As a teenager I hated him so much. The last year or so, I thought I'd come to understand him. I wanted to come out to both my parents. I almost did this Christmas. I wanted to so bad. I discovered I needed their approval more than I thought. I wanted to end the pressure of hiding so much of my life. Living one place with them thinking I was somewhere else. It was awful. I pictured myself sometimes, talking to my dad for hours, convincing him, and he'd realize he'd been wrong about gay people. Now, that will never happen."

Mike snuffled the snot in his nose for a moment and then resumed. "I said lots of hateful things that I can't take back. I didn't wait for his answer. I just turned around and left him there. I went back to the dressing room. When I came out for my last set, he was gone."

Turner unlocked the handcuffs. Mike wiped his face with his hanky. He looked at the two detectives.

Turner said, "We have a source who says he saw you with your dad at the Kennedy Federal Building."

"That's not true."

Turner almost believed him. Here was a gay kid in pain, who'd just had his father murdered, and he wanted to believe the son had nothing to do with it, but his cop instincts told him the kid's last statement was a lie.

Fenwick said, "You'll be in the film from the security camera at the Federal Building."

"It wasn't me."

"You were angry enough to kill your dad," Fenwick stated.

"But I didn't."

"What did you do after work that morning?" Turner asked.

"I came back here. The next day I was in and out. I called my answering machine in Bloomington from here to get my messages. That's how I knew I was supposed to call my mom."

"Dana Sickles said you didn't have a phone," Turner said. He glanced around the apartment. "I don't see one."

"I have a cellular phone. I wanted as few people as possible knowing where I was. I didn't want even an unlisted number here."

"Why did your father follow you around town? Why didn't he simply go back home?"

"I'm not sure. I'd told him about the bar, and that I was going to work. My father always did what he felt like doing. He was the ruler of the roost. It was a very Republican thing, he was more important than anyone else, so he should always get his way in what was best for him."

"We're going to have to hold you until after we look at the film from the camera at the Federal Building," Turner said.

"I wasn't there."

Fenwick asked, "Did you kill your dad?"

"No."

"Why did you run from us earlier?" Turner asked.

"Maybe I'm not as bright as I think I am."

16

They put him in the backseat of the unmarked car and drove to the rear entrance of Area Ten Headquarters to avoid any reporters out front. They almost got the kid upstairs unnoticed, but a stray reporter standing at the front desk spotted them.

"Hey!" he yelled. He ran toward them. "Have you arrested Judge Meade's son? What's going on?"

People gaped at them. Turner and Mike Meade continued up the stairs. Fenwick barred the reporter's progress.

"Why are you bringing him up the back way?"

"To avoid any questions from dopes like you," Fenwick said.

"Why are you avoiding questions?"

"Look," Fenwick said, "he's helping us with the investigation. We're taking all the help we can get. What's wrong with the son helping us?"

"I think I've got a scoop."

Acting Commander Molton hurried down the stairs. "Problem here?" he asked.

"Why have the police arrested Judge Meade's son?"

Molton said, "No one has been arrested. No arrest is imminent. We are getting help from as many people as possible." Molton drew the reporter away from Fenwick, allowing the detective to hustle up the stairs as fast as his bulk would allow. As Fenwick climbed, he heard Molton making soothing noises at the reporter.

On the third floor Turner was hunting in a storage room for a VCR that worked. He'd already rolled a cart with a television on it next to their desks.

"Where's the kid?" Fenwick asked.

"I arrested him."

"Funny."

"I proposed marriage, and he said yes."

"Unlikely."

"He died."

Fenwick said, "You've got him on the fourth floor in one of the conference rooms."

"If you knew that, why did you ask?"

"Habit? I wanted to exercise my jaw? I want to win the Carruthers-Is-Stupid prize?"

Turner walked out with a VCR. He brought it over to the television and rested the VCR on the shelf below the television on the cart. He plugged the machines in, hooked them up, put in one of the tapes, and pressed play. Turner and Fenwick placed their chairs so they could both watch it at the same time.

They recognized the empty corridor as that of the Kennedy Federal Building. In the distance they could see cars going by on Dearborn Street. The film had a time display/counter in the lower-right-hand corner.

Nothing moved in the corridor. "This is boring," Fenwick said. He picked up the remote control and pressed fast forward. Twice they saw the security man, Leo Kramer, doing a high-speed Charlie Chan imitation. The guard never looked up at the camera, but his general body structure and his little white goatee made it evident that it was he.

Rodriguez walked up behind Turner and Fenwick. He watched the screen for a few minutes as the film of the empty corridor whizzed by. He said, "I've seen this before. The bad guys get caught, but before they do, they rescue a baby whale from evil adventurers so, before the hero machine-guns them, he forgives them."

"That's the sequel," Turner said, "this is the original."

Rodriguez stooped closer and peered at the screen. "I think you're right," he said. "You guys hear who won the pool?"

"No," Fenwick said.

"It just got announced downstairs. Some uniform on the admitting desk is up five hundred bucks. It was some nerdy blond named O'Leary who's been out of the academy less than a month. There is no justice."

"Life's like that," Fenwick said.

"You're cute when you're profound," Rodriguez said. He pointed at the television set. "Much as I hate to miss any of this, anybody seen what's-his-name? Molton told me I wasn't supposed to let him out of my sight."

Turner and Fenwick shook their heads. They knew he meant Carruthers. Rodriguez wandered away.

They watched seven full tapes of nothing flash by. A third of the way into the eighth, a figure hurried out of the building. Turner stopped the tape and ran it backward. He put it on normal speed and let it run. They saw a well-muffled man with his back to the camera. All the film showed was that he came in to the camera's range and walked out the door.

Turner pressed freeze frame. "This is who?"

Fenwick put his face inches from the screen. "Can't tell really. Sort of has Mike Meade's build."

"Time says nine thirty-nine."

"Kid said his dad followed him to the bar."

"No, he said he presumed he followed him. He looked up from his dancing and there he was."

"So, dad and son took a side trip to the Federal Building. Why?"

"Or the kid is lying."

"We'll have to ask him."

"I've got that list from Janice Caldwell."

Turner opened his briefcase, shuffled through several papers, and came out with the list. He glanced down it. "Note here says no one had signed in. She didn't know who this was." Turner peered at the screen and checked his notes. "The time's about right. I don't see another person. Carl Schurz said he heard voices, plural. I only see one person hurrying out."

"Schurz lied or the tapes are totally screwed up."

"I'm not going to court with this as identification."

"Tell me there isn't another way in or out."

"Caldwell says all the exits and entrances have security cameras, but only one was supposed to be unlocked at that time. We should have everything, but she was double-checking." Turner reached for the phone and dialed the Kennedy Federal Building. When he got through to Caldwell, he asked about other possible exits.

"In those tapes you have," she said, "there's supposed to be one of a small private elevator the judges can use to go directly to the parking garage. They have a special section reserved for them. They don't have to check in or out. You have to have a special card to enter or exit. You just insert the card, and the gate goes up and you can enter or leave. You don't have to pay."

"Meade could have gone out that way?"

"Or in," Caldwell said. "You could also walk in through the parking garage."

"There was more than one entrance unlocked?"

"I'm sorry, yes. I should have made it clearer sooner. If you aren't in a car, you don't need a card to open the gate. It's a bit of walk, inconvenient, but not difficult."

"We didn't find any tapes of a back elevator."

"You were supposed to have them. I've checked here carefully. I'll look again, but if you don't have them, that probably means the tapes are gone. Or maybe they were never working."

"Or someone tampered with them or took them."

"Maybe, but as you know, we've had glitches with this building. For a week, the metal-scanning device at the entrance worked only sporadically. We had to use hand-held scanners. The lines were horrendous. It could simply be gone or never been working in the first place."

"You can't mean you're missing a whole series of tapes."

Turner glanced at Fenwick and shook his head.

"Missing or never taken. Either way, I'm sorry. I'm sure they aren't here, but I promise I'll check again."

Turner told Fenwick the news.

"Maybe Leo Kramer took them and destroyed them," Fenwick said.

"Possible."

"Who's in charge of them?"

"Caldwell claimed she'd investigate."

"Maybe she's covering up for somebody," Fenwick suggested.

"For who?"

"One of the judges?"

"Wadsworth or Malmsted come to mind. One of them the killer? Or maybe they're in a conspiracy?"

"Don't start that conspiracy shit," Fenwick said. "I hate conspiracy shit. There are no conspiracies. It's just assholes being stupid."

"I don't picture Caldwell being part of some evil cabal. She seemed solid, sensible."

"So, maybe Carl Schurz wasn't lying. We'll have to find him to ask him which entrance he was near."

"Maybe this isn't Meade?"

"Who then?"

Turner shrugged.

Carruthers bustled into the room and hurried over to them. "I hear you guys arrested Judge Meade's son. It's on all the newscasts. The kid did it. Wow! Can you prove it? You better be careful. Look what happened to those cops in LA when they screwed up a high-profile case."

Fenwick stood up, put his arm around Carruthers' shoulder, and shouted directly into his ear, "Fuck off."

Carruthers jumped. He backed away. "Hey, what'd you do that for? I was just trying to be friendly and supportive." He cupped his hand over his ear, listened for a moment, and shook his head. "I think you hurt something permanently." He twisted a finger in his ear. "Hey, that wasn't very nice. I was trying to help." He stalked away.

"I think I may have gone a bit far that time," Fenwick said.

Turner said, "You'll have to apologize."

"No."

"I think so."

Fenwick grumbled deep in his throat, "After this case is over."

They went back to viewing the tapes. The only person who wasn't a security guard was at that one spot. For half an hour, frame by frame, they ran that portion of the tape backwards and forwards. They got no nearer to identification than before.

"Let's turn this over to the electronics experts at Eleventh and State," Turner said. "Maybe they can get something. For all we know they may have the dates or timing wrong. Somebody could have doctored it. Maybe this isn't what we needed at all."

Fenwick nodded agreement.

"We let the kid go?" Turner asked.

"We have a choice?"

Turner shook his head.

They met with Mike Meade in the gray-painted conference room on the fourth floor.

"Are you going to let me go?" Meade asked.

"If your dad followed you to the bar, how come we have you on tape at the Federal Building?"

"You couldn't have. I wasn't there. Let me see it."

They took him to the third floor and showed him. "That could be anybody."

"You said he followed you."

"That's what I figured. I wasn't monitoring his movements that night. I just went to work."

He stuck with that story and a half hour of questioning got them no further.

Minutes later they hustled Mike Meade into the back of an unmarked car. They took him to his mother's house. They said little to each other on the way over.

On the return trip Turner said, "I still think he's lying."

"Sure is possible. We've got to prove it."

"We've got to find Carl Schurz."

17

Fenwick pulled off Lake Shore Drive at Wacker and took it west. Lower Wacker Drive, one of the fastest ways around downtown Chicago, made a half circle a level below surface streets from southwest to northeast around the Loop. Open on one side to the Chicago River, the other side contained a warren of underground nooks, crannies, and deadfalls to crawl into, fall down, or die in—the basements, garbage bins, and secret recesses of the steel and concrete behemoths that soared above the streets.

They found the corner Roman Ayres had told them Carl Schurz or his dope dealer might inhabit. They saw several abandoned refrigerator cartons, wind-whipped bits of cardboard, plastic paper wrapping, and torn fast-food containers around the darkened area. The lights on lower Wacker Drive seemed more to infringe on the darkness than to provide illumination. They found the opening Ayres had indicated.

The passage was dim and sloped slightly downward. The wind died at the entrance to the narrow walkway. They stepped over the leavings of the homeless: rolled-up newspapers, grime-encrusted towels, rusting outdoor grills, yellow-and-brown-stained mattresses, empty tin cans, cold embers of fires never warm enough in the first place to keep the Chicago winter at bay.

About twenty feet farther on they came to an opening. If people were doing drugs, it wasn't here. This space may have been out of the direct wind, but it was still bitterly cold. Near the rear of this collective hovel, an air shaft led up to street level far above. It let in the only light, street dimness from high overhead. Garbage covered the entire floor of the thirty-by-twenty living area. As far as Turner could tell, this could be the Ritz for the homeless. Fenwick and Turner began poking their way through the debris. Turner didn't expect to find anything, at the same time he feared what they might. Near the back they found a baby carriage a child might use for its dolls. Inside were tattered doll-size clothes neatly folded.

"My butt is almost frozen," Fenwick said.

"Let's at least hunt through the larger mounds of stuff. Hate to think the kid crawled in here tonight."

"I don't like it that no one else is around," Fenwick said. "Makes me shiver, and not from the cold."

Fenwick began prodding the largest mound of debris in the corner under the best light while Turner unearthed mounds of garbage near the baby carriage.

Fenwick said, "Carl Schurz is going to make a very poor witness."

"He was probably lying," Turner said. "Won't be surprised if he denies everything."

"Lying witnesses I don't like," Fenwick said, "but dead ones depress me. You better come here." Fenwick pulled away several layers of cardboard.

The body looked like it was sleeping peacefully. Turner took off his gloves, leaned down, and touched the face. Carl Schurz was dead.

Fenwick returned to the car to call for backup. Turner remained standing over the body. "You poor kid," he muttered at the body and the cement walls. "Nobody ever loved you enough, or maybe there was never enough love to give you, or maybe you weren't very lovable. And there was nothing any of us could have done about it." The cold seeped into his consciousness and prevented further emotional speculation. Almost automatically, Turner began the investigation.

Turner and Fenwick and the technicians inspected the area carefully. They found several needles and less than an ounce of marijuana. They could find no wounds on Schurz's body. The ME said he'd get to the autopsy as quickly as possible.

"I thought Lower Wacker cleared out when it got this cold," Turner said to one of the uniformed cops.

"Usually does. We know a lot of drugs go down around here. We try to clean it out. They always find some place. They seem to be able to sense if something has gone wrong."

"Did he die from the cold or someone kill him?" Turner asked the ME.

"Not sure. Probably cold, just like a lot of the other homeless."

"Maybe he just got tired of living," Turner said. "Crawled into a hole and let himself die."

"We're all freezing our butts off," one of the Crime Lab people said. "Let's blow this dump. He was just a homeless dead kid."

"He's not just a homeless dead kid," Turner said. "His life was important. It made a difference that he was alive." Turner felt awkward defending Carl Schurz. He also wished that what he'd said was true.

Turner went through the pockets. He pulled out a wallet. He would inspect it back at Headquarters.

In the car on the way back to Area Ten, Turner said, "I'm really pissed. He shouldn't be dead. There was no reason for him to be on the streets. There are places he could have gone for help."

"You're taking this hard," Fenwick said.

"He was a troubled gay kid. He didn't have to die. He was bright, nice looking. Not that long ago, he was an innocent little kid, playing with toys, asking somebody to read him a book, trying to get a little attention in the best way he could, just like the rest of us. I'm going to see Ian. Maybe he knows something about what happened."

"Why not call him and talk first?" Fenwick asked. "He'd have phoned us if he'd seen the kid."

"I guess I'll call."

"Paul, why aren't we considering Ian a suspect?"

Paul stared out the window in silence.

"Paul?"

"I've thought of it. He isn't the killer."

"You mean he didn't do it, or you hope he didn't do it?"

"Both."

"He's known a lot of information from mysterious sources. I don't like mysterious sources."

"I know," Paul said. "My years of friendship with him and all that I know about him says he wouldn't kill."

"Anybody's capable of it."

"Yeah."

Fenwick let the subject drop. Back in the squad room, someone had had pizza delivered. Turner tried a piece and almost choked on it. Even Fenwick found his prodigious appetite blunted.

Turner went through the wallet. There were two driver's licenses, both made out to Carl Schurz. One said he was sixteen, the other that he was twenty-one. One address was for Lubbock, Texas, the other for Rapid City, South Dakota. He found an identification card for the Kennedy Federal Building. Schurz had two dollars in change. No social security card, no credit cards, no voter registration, no medical card, no pictures, no hidden compartments with keys or addresses.

He called both cities. Lubbock had one listing for a Jack Schurz. Turner realized it was near midnight, but he phoned anyway. The person who answered said he didn't know any Carl Schurz. He sounded like he'd been asleep. He gave brief, terse answers to Turner's questions. The Rapid City operator had no listing for any Schurz. Turner wondered—had the parents moved away, had a smart kid gotten two fake IDs? He suspected that the one that identified him as sixteen and dated the year before was the accurate one.

Turner tried to do paperwork, but his mind wouldn't focus. He was used to death, but Carl Schurz was different. He'd touched him, held him, felt the kid's needs. He didn't think he could have ever met them.

Turner gave up writing reports. He picked up and began reading one of the dissents the judge had written in an abortion case. After two paragraphs he put it down. He wasn't sure if it made sense or not. Right now, he didn't care.

Molton entered the room. He said, "I heard you got bad news."

"We've had a fucked-up day," Fenwick said.

"It's tough to lose a witness in a murder case," Molton said.

"We're not sure what he knew," Fenwick said.

They discussed the case with him for several minutes. After he left, Turner tried calling Ian at home. There was no answer, so he tried his private number at the paper. Ian picked up on the third ring.

"It's Paul. Carl Schurz is dead."

Ian was silent.

"You there?" Turner asked.

"Yeah." Ian's voice was subdued. "What happened?"

Turner explained.

Ian said, "There was no reason that kid had to die."

"I know."

"What can I do?"

"I don't know. I wanted to tell you."

"Thanks. I doubt if anybody knows any family. If I can't find anyone, I'll try and work it out so that he gets some kind of decent burial. Maybe his parents put out a missing kid's notice?"

"I put in a search on him. Nothing turned up. If they threw him out, they wouldn't turn in a report."

"This is such shit," Ian said. "Goddamn kids don't need to die."

"I'm tired and depressed," Turner said.

They were silent for several moments. Finally Ian said, "How badly does this hurt your investigation?"

"I'm not sure. Geary says the judge was at Au Naturel. Schurz confirms and adds information about the Federal Building. Now he's gone. The son gave us more details. Maybe we wouldn't need Schurz after all. Hurting the case is a pain in the ass, but that boy should not have died."

Ian agreed, but there was nothing either one could do at the moment.

"Why are you still at the paper?" Turner asked.

"Working on the Meade case. I've been at it eighteen hours a day. If you need to talk, let's meet."

"In an hour or so. I'm going to stop at the autopsy."

Turner thanked him and hung up. He stared at the papers strewn on the top of his desk, the remnants of pizza next to the space heater by his feet, then back at Fenwick. His friend met his gaze.

"Time to go home," Fenwick said. "We're not going to get any more done tonight."

"I guess."

Fenwick had never heard his friend sound so defeated. "You okay?" he asked.

"Yeah, sure."

Fenwick gazed at him carefully. "That sounds more like you mean you're not okay, but you don't want to talk about it."

Turner really liked Fenwick, but at the moment he wanted to talk to a gay person about what had happened to Carl Schurz. Fenwick was a good friend, probably his best nongay friend, but sometimes you needed to talk to one of your own, someone who had shared the strains of being a gay person in America at the tail end of the twentieth century.

Turner gave Fenwick a brief smile. "I'm going to be fine. You're right. Let's call it a day. I'm going to stop at the morgue, see if they started the autopsy."

"Want me to go with?"

"If they find anything important, I'll call you."

Outside the wind was dead calm. Turner could feel the cold against his face. The weather bureau predicted the temperature would hit twenty below zero by midnight but then begin to climb before morning. The prediction was for near freezing by the end of the weekend.

After he started the motor, Turner shivered in his car for a few minutes. He watched Fenwick pull away. He needed to get home. He hadn't seen Jeff or Ben all day. Ben would have long since picked up Jeff and brought him back to the house. He wanted to feel the warmth of his home, his family, and the arms of his lover, but he couldn't get Carl Schurz out of his mind.

Turner drove over to Cook County Morgue. He walked past the half-tile, half-glass entry room. A body lay there on a gurney waiting for transportation to the back. He walked down the corridor toward the autopsy room. As always, the room was pristine clean except where they were doing the current autopsy. Every surface was gleaming stainless steel.

The ME working on the body looked up. It was Hamilton Trout, who was short, stout, black-haired, and enormously competent. At the moment Hamilton was holding a liver in his left hand. Turner looked at the face on the table. It was Schurz. The body cavity gaped open. The naked corpse looked waxen, cold, dead. The ME weighed the liver and placed it carefully on a table.

"This one yours?" Hamilton asked.

"Yeah." Turner wasn't exceptionally squeamish after all these years of viewing autopsies. He was not ready, however, to jump into a vat of corpses either. He approached the body. He noted the smell. Same as all the others, chemicals and body odors.

"You know how he died?" Turner asked.

"Think so. Freezing was the immediate cause of death, but not the first cause."

"Come again?"

"Kid was on his way to being very dead. He'd taken enough

pills to put himself away. If somebody would have found him before he froze, they probably could have saved him. A little stomach pump and he's fine. He took more than enough to ease whatever pain he was in, crawled into the cold, fell asleep, and died."

"Killed himself."

"Tried to. Cold finished it for him."

"You're sure?"

"Pretty much. I've got more tests to run, but that's my best guess now. I doubt if it's going to change. Does the way he died make a difference to what you're working on?" As he spoke, the ME began examining and weighing more organs. Sometimes he paused to cut off bits of tissue to be labeled, stored, and examined more thoroughly later.

"No, no difference. It bothers me that there's another dead gay kid."

"He was gay?" Hamilton pointed at the body. "Can't tell it from the corpse."

"No difference when we're dead. He a drug addict?"

"No needle tracks anywhere. I'll have to check for other drugs. You know this kid?"

"Only briefly as a witness."

"Some bother you more than others."

"Yeah. Something else comes up, let me know."

"Sure."

Paul met Ian at the Melrose Restaurant on Broadway. They sat in the corner front booth. Watching the parade of hot men stroll past was one of the great joys of a summer evening spent in this booth. Now, at midnight on a bitterly cold Saturday in January, the streets were mostly deserted. Traffic was sparse and pedestrians nonexistent.

Ian was already there. Paul tossed his hat, coat, gloves, and scarf onto the seat. He ordered soup and salad.

After the waitress left, he turned to Ian and said, "Schurz committed suicide."

Ian shook his head, stirred his coffee, sipped it. Put it down, dumped a packet of sugar in it, and stirred again. He said, "Too many gay kids die." For years, Ian had been working on a series of articles on gay kids and suicide. Some studies indicated that from thirty to forty percent of teens who tried to kill themselves were gay. Ian hadn't been able to prove or disprove that statistic, but he'd researched the deaths of a lot of gay kids over the years.

"You knew this one personally," Turner said.

"That makes it all the harder. It's depressing and makes me angry. I thought about it since you called. You know, this is the first one in all these years that I actually knew."

"Really?"

"All the others were statistics. I listened to disembodied voices of relatives over phone lines trying to cope with tragedy. Sometimes I got overworked cops in distant cities or reporters trying to make their own headlines and deadlines. A few people I contacted, straight and gay, were sensitive to the needs of frightened, suicidal gay teens. These kids are drowning in misery before they're twenty. They're mostly invisible, and they die with nothing to show for their lives."

"Mike Meade's fondest wish was that he not be gay," Turner said.

"He told you that?"

"Yep."

"Hell of a world we live in. Too many gay kids learn self-hatred."

Their food arrived. "I didn't find much among Carl Schurz's things," Turner said. He explained what little he had found in the wallet. "I tried calling both addresses. Whether they were fake or real, nobody at the other end knew a Carl Schurz. Maybe the one in Lubbock wasn't fake. It was kind of late to be calling. Guy thought it was strange when I asked him his age. He asked me if I was really a cop. Finally told me he was twenty-two."

"Not going to be the daddy."

"No. I wonder where Carl was really from? Where are his parents? Will they ever know he's dead?"

"I never knew where he came from. He kept a lot of secrets. When you're a gay kid, you learn from an early age how to hide important feelings, important information. You know that as well as I do. A gay or lesbian kid may not be a consummate liar, but, unless they are very lucky, they better be very good at disguise."

They each ate for a few minutes. The soup, as always, was delicious. The warmth revived Turner slightly.

Ian said, "I didn't find out anything new today. I couldn't find Carl. Maybe if I would have . . ." His voice trailed off. He was silent for a moment then said, "It's easy to get lost in Chicago. I wonder if he was telling the truth about what he saw on New Year's Eve."

"I'd like to find out."

"My sources are dried up. I've called half of my Rolodex and some of those two or three times. I've snooped every place I know of in the gay community. Nothing. No Carl today. No information from anybody."

"That's about the same as we got today."

"Maybe if I hadn't convinced Carl to talk to you, he wouldn't be dead."

"Maybe's can kill you," Paul said. "You've told me that hundreds of times."

"Just because it's my excellent advice, doesn't mean I have to take it."

"Gay kids are going to keep dying."

"Yes, and so are gay adults. A teacher friend called the other day. He'd found a note that fell out of a book a kid had left behind in his classroom. The note said that all the kids knew that the teacher was gay, and the boy's dad said all gay people should have a bullet hole put in their heads. This from a sophomore in high school."

"Did the teacher report it?"

"He didn't dare. He's not openly gay at school."

"The kids know, but he's not out?"

"It's one thing to be gay, it's another to talk about it. If you tell your administrator, you might force him or her to act."

Paul nodded. "You know I'm not the kind to feel sorry for myself, but at the moment I sure feel put upon by the world. I'm depressed, and I feel like shit."

"I know what you mean, but do remember a hefty dose of self-pity can be good for the soul. If you're not going to feel sorry for yourself, who is, and frankly who is better at feeling sorry for yourself, than you?"

Paul smiled briefly. He finished his food in silence. He took great comfort in the simple closeness of his friend. They paid and left.

At home Paul found Ben asleep on the couch. Quietly, he hung his winter outer garments in the entryway closet. Paul checked on Jeff. He sat on the side of his son's bed. He stroked Jeff's hair gently, pulled the covers up carefully, and leaned over and placed a kiss on his son's forehead.

In the kitchen, he found several messages. One was from Rose Talucci. Another said that Brian had called and sent his love. Paul wished his older son was home. He heard footsteps in the hallway. Moments later Ben walked into the kitchen.

"You're home?" Ben sounded groggy from sleep.

Paul walked up to his lover. He enfolded him in his arms. Ben returned the embrace. The feel of his lover's arms on his back, his torso against his own, soothed Paul. This was what he needed—the few moments of human contact. He kept his arm around Ben's waist as they ascended the stairs to bed. They undressed slowly and slid between the covers. Paul put his head on his lover's chest. "Just hold me," he whispered. Ben's hands rested on his side and back. Paul drew a deep breath. He fell asleep moments later.

18

"You feeling any better?" Fenwick asked Turner the next morning as they waited for roll call to start.

"I had a talk with Ian and got a chance to be home. I'm working on being pissed off mixed with resignation in the face of hopeless reality."

"The day's early. You'll get over it."

Acting Commander Molton drew them aside after the morning formalities. "Pressure is starting to get intense. The interest in this case is not going to go away. What have you got?"

They told him of yesterday's developments.

"The inquiry is going backward," Molton said. He shook his head. "Whatever you need around here is yours. I got a call from the Justice Department this morning. The mayor's office phoned my home last night. The Federal Bureau of Investigation is pestering me, and the superintendent wants to meet with me for an update. This is getting ugly. Get out there and get me something."

They hustled to their desks. On top of the pile of paperwork, Turner found a note that said call the airlines. He did. The official, a youthful-sounding male, told him that Judge Meade's luggage had turned up. Turner listened to him explain that, especially on international flights, anyone who checks in luggage but doesn't board the plane sets off an alarm in security. The luggage was removed, examined, and placed in storage. The paperwork hadn't surfaced on his desk until today. The official also told Turner that, except for his return flight, they had no record of a second airline ticket for the judge.

"Could he have flown under another name?" Turner asked.

"Very doubtful," the man said. "It used to be that if you paid cash, you could fly domestically under any name you wanted. Not any more. On any flight, crossing international borders, whatever, you've got to have identification."

After he hung up, Turner told Fenwick this.

"So he really planned to go?" Fenwick asked.

"Got to be. First, the judge checks in, then he sees the kid and his world changes. Maybe he really planned to go."

"So, The judge was really on his way to Canada. Which would mean the trip was not a huge cover-up and he was not a closet case. So, we know one thing; he wasn't gay. He sees his kid. Is one kiss going to stop the judge from saying hello and cause him to cancel a trip?"

"I think it is safe to say that something stopped him from making the trip," Turner said. "Precisely what? We've got what the kid says, but how far do we believe him? I don't think we got the whole truth from him."

"I don't either. What if Mike Meade and his dad had a fight in the airport? We got the report from the uniforms who talked to people out there?"

Turner hunted through the piles of paper and found the paperwork. He glanced over it. "They interviewed the personnel at the check-in counter, at the gate, and on the plane. The woman at the counter didn't remember the judge. Nobody noticed him at the gate. They're willing to give us the passenger list. We could call all the people on the flight in the hopes someone saw him."

"Put some uniforms on it. We probably should try all the people on the kid's flight too."

"Right. They talked to the people in the shops on the concourse the plane flew from. No one remembers him."

"One of the busiest flying days of the year. Lucky if they remember their own name."

"They could have had the fight right there, or maybe there was no fight. We only have his word for it that he came in at the airport or that he met his dad there. I'm starting to doubt everything. Maybe Geary is wrong about seeing the judge. Schurz was unreliable. Maybe Mike Meade is making everything up."

"Try this," Fenwick said. "Kid and dad argue at the airport then get in a cab to go home. The argument gets out of control. The cabby conveniently looks the other way as the kid pulls out gun he has flown in with on an airplane and blows his dad away. The cabby obligingly keeps the dead body in the car until two in the morning."

"If we believe the body arrived with the noises heard by the bookstore owner down the street. Your scenario leaves a mite to be desired."

"Yeah, I can't see a cab driver not charging a fortune for the ride. Nobody could afford it. Let me try again. They really do argue, but they go someplace else to do it. They don't want to go home, let's not upset Mom."

"Why not? Is Mom that fragile?"

"We have no proof of that."

"They argue somewhere else?"

"Kid's apartment up north?" Turner asked.

"I didn't see any blood. Would he want his dad to know he had a secret place?"

"Along with a secret life?"

"So they argue someplace, the Federal Building?"

"Why there?"

"Why not? The kid gets a gun from somewhere. After he shoots Dad, he drops the weapon down a convenient storm drain. He gets to work on time, but just before he starts dancing, he puts his dad in a convenient dumpster near the bar where he is leading a double life."

"Kid says he doesn't own a car," Turner said. "How's he

going to be dragging his dad around? I'm having trouble buying Mike Meade as the killer."

"Should we search the Meade home and the kid's apartment here and in Bloomington?"

"Do we have enough evidence for search warrants?"

"Kid claims to have seen his dad the night of the murder."

"So did Geary. Are we going to search his place? Carl Schurz had no place to search."

"We have to call the airlines and confirm they had a Mike Meade fly in that night."

Fenwick reached for his phone and began punching in numbers. Turner called the Department of Motor Vehicles and gave them Mike Meade's name and address. They had no record of him owning a car in Illinois.

A moment after Turner hung up, his phone rang. It was the commander of the police district Au Naturel was in.

"Sorry I didn't get back to you sooner," the commander said. "Heard you had a question about activity here."

"Yeah, some pretty raw stuff goes on in Au Naturel."

"Bar on Lincoln Avenue?"

"Yeah."

"I get no complaints. I don't act unless I get a complaint. Their license is up to date. Probably pay their taxes on time."

"You've had no problems there?"

"None."

After Fenwick got off the phone, Turner told him what the commander had said.

"Which means Dana Sickles paid her graft on time?" Fenwick asked.

"She's obviously in good with the local commander. I've sometimes wondered how some of those dancers get away with some of the things they wear or don't wear. Those fishnet jockstraps a few of them parade around in can't be completely legal."

"Did you want to file a complaint?"

"No."

"For whatever reason, the local commander doesn't hassle her. Maybe it's simply because she runs a clean place, does pay her bills, doesn't get complaints, and is an upstanding, outstanding member of the community."

"She's a Republican. Maybe the commander's a Republican too. Aren't they all paragons of civic virtue?"

Fenwick said, "I'm the only paragon around here. The airlines confirm that a Mike Meade flew from St. Louis to Chicago on New Year's Eve. The flight was late three hours."

"And the truth shall set you free."

Rodriguez entered the room. His hand was on the elbow of a uniformed cop. Turner thought he looked more like he was leading a possible suspect than a co-worker. Together they trudged over to Turner. The young cop was tall, blond-haired, and handsome. His uniform pants clung to his narrow hips.

They stopped in front of Turner. The young cop hung his head and muttered in a rush, "I'm sorry about the phone call you got the other day. I didn't know it was important. If I did something wrong, I apologize."

"Which phone call?" Turner asked.

"You got a personal call wondering if you were all right."

This was the guy who had been rude to Ben. Turner read his identification badge—Jason O'Leary, the guy who won the betting pool the day before.

Fenwick got up, moved next to the man, and placed one of his huge arms around the guy's shoulders. "A self-confessed homophobic creep." He squeezed the guy's shoulder. "I always wanted to see one of those in person."

"Lay off." O'Leary shrugged off Fenwick's hand.

Turner shook his head at Fenwick. His partner dropped his arm.

Rodriguez said, "See, confession is good for the soul. You feel better?"

The uniform muttered, "I need to go."

"Then get the hell out," Rodriguez said.

The three of them watched the guy walk out.

"Thanks, I think," Turner said.

"He's an asshole," Rodriguez said, "and he's starting to screw up as much as Carruthers. He's the nephew of a good friend of mine up in the Twenty-third. I figured I'd set him straight."

"How'd you find out what was going on?" Turner asked Rodriguez.

Fenwick said, "I mentioned it. Figured it was okay."

Turner nodded.

"You'll never guess how I got on to him." Rodriguez leaned closer. "Don't spread this around, but it was Carruthers."

Turner and Fenwick gawked at him.

Rodriguez smiled at their looks. "Don't get me wrong. He didn't deliberately help out. We were at a gang killing and he was talking to some buddies. I overheard one of the beat cops telling him a story about getting even with a faggot detective.

"I kind of wandered over. To give him credit, Carruthers wasn't happy about what the guy said. Almost defended you, Paul."

"Damn," Fenwick said. "Do we give him a medal?"

Carruthers bustled into the room and over to them. He saw them staring and looked from one to the other. "What?" he asked. Carruthers wore an aviator's hat complete with ear flaps, a sweater with cigarette burn holes in it, and a maroon leather coat that hung almost to his knees.

"Thanks, Randy," Turner said.

"For what?"

"O'Leary was just up here apologizing."

Carruthers said, "I know you're a homosexual. I don't believe in special rights for anybody, but I don't believe anybody should have to put up with prejudice. I know the time my mom tried to call, when she thought I'd been shot, she was frantic. Nobody who loves you should be treated like that. It's not fair and it's not right. I know you guys don't like me and laugh at me and I don't expect any favors for this, but what that guy said was wrong. It was the right thing to do, to make him come apologize."

Turner didn't remember Miss Manners guide to responding appropriately to those who've defended you when you least expected it.

Turner said, "Thanks again, Randy."

"You don't owe me," Carruthers said. "What's right is right." He left.

"Isn't that precious," Fenwick said. "The least likely person on the planet doing you a favor."

"I don't like feeling obliged to him."

"You're not obliged to him or me," Rodriguez said. "Asshole O'Leary might have learned something. I better go chase down my partner. Doing one good thing might give him ideas."

Turner thanked Rodriguez. He left.

"That really was good of Carruthers," Turner said, "but it feels funny. Kind of like winning the grand prize everybody's talking about, but it turns out to be two weeks in Newton, Iowa. Weird. Somebody who's supposed to be a dope doing something pretty goddamn nice, but with mildly offensive overtones."

"Maybe he wanted you to feel obligated?"

"Does Carruthers' thinking get to that level?"

"What if I'd done it?" Fenwick asked.

"I don't know. For some reason, I think it would have been funnier. Could we have been wrong about Carruthers all this time?"

"No," Fenwick said.

Fenwick sat down at his desk. "Now what?" he asked.

"We catch up on the rest of the reports we haven't read yet." Turner lifted up the pile on his desk. "Nothing flagged here, presumably nothing anybody found significant. Might as well hunt through them now."

They found the Crime Lab report concerning the back door at Au Naturel. A little vomit, a little beer, fifty-seven different partial finger and/or thumb prints. No blood on the door, the floor, or anywhere on the property in the backyard of the bar. Turner found the section on the blood in the alley. The samples from the ground matched those of the dead man.

The contents of the dumpster the body was found in included the normal detritus of an urban alley, but nary a thing unusual or that seemed even remotely to be a clue.

Turner said, "I want to talk to Geary, Sickles, and Meade. I want lots of information about the judge's son. Mike Meade must have friends. I want complete background on him and the same with the rest of the family. I also want to talk to the judge who Albert Meade most agreed with."

After half an hour Fenwick tossed his stack onto his desk. "This is crap."

"Who's working on the judge's decisions?"

Fenwick hunted. "Some uniform named Sangri Di Cristo."

It took them five minutes of wading through several levels of bureaucrats to find out that the woman they wanted to talk to was one flight above them on the fourth floor.

Turner thought she must be in her midtwenties. She smiled at them. In her tiny office the space heater was going full blast. Her desk was pristinely neat. One large stack of papers was to her left. A ten-page report was open in front of her. Immediately to the right of this was a pad of lined white paper. Farther to her right was a smaller stack of files. She had one pink and one blue highlighter on the desk. Next to them was a black ballpoint pen. Turner saw several lines of the document underlined in pink.

She smiled at them. They asked what she had.

Di Cristo picked up her pad of paper and flipped back to the front. Turner saw that she printed in precise block letters.

She said, "First, I started with the opinions the judge was supposed to have written himself. I began with the first one and read through them. I believe he basically wrote them all himself."

"Barlow claimed he wrote them," Turner said.

"That tight-assed twit made a lot of claims," Fenwick said.

She continued, "Clerks come and go and you would notice changes in style. Very few alterations, and those that are there are very minor. Second, logic, reasoning, and knowledge of the law. They put me on this because I'm going through law school. I am not an absolute expert, but from what I've seen, the logic holds together, the reasoning is generally sound, knowledge of the law okay. At least a B-plus communicator on paper. Third, types of decisions he worked on—mostly they were noncontroversial. The kind people never hear about—mundane and boring. Nothing really spectacular. Fourth, the controversial decisions. They were almost invariably written by Judge Horatio G. Wright, who has been on this circuit six months longer than Meade was. His writing is brilliant. If you accept his premises, then you cannot disagree with him. He is good. One oddity, Meade wrote all the decisions concerning gay people. That's all I have so far. I can give you a full report tomorrow around noon."

Turner said, "Judge Malmsted told us he was stupid."

"I can't say that based on what I've read so far."

"They hated each other," Fenwick said.

Sangri said, "Perhaps her view of her colleague was a bit jaundiced because of that."

"Could be," Turner said.

They thanked her and left. On the way down the stairs Fenwick said, "I hate it when people are that organized and neat. I think it must be a character defect."

"They've been slipping on that lately at the academy. I heard they dropped Intermediate and Advanced Slob."

"They still do teach Introductory Chaos 101 and 102?"

"Certainly, but obviously some slip by."

"Summary executions might help," Fenwick said.

"I want her on all the cases I have to do research on."

"She won't be a cop long."

"Now that we're armed with better questions, let's go see Judge Horatio G. Wright."

"Hell of a name for a judge."

"Sounds more like the name of a Civil War general to me."

"You're thinking of Horace Greely," Fenwick said.

"I am?"

"We've interviewed nearly seventy people in the past few days. Which one was he?"

"Horace Greely was a newspaperman back in . . ."

"I am not amused. I'm sure whichever one Horatio was, he must be in our notes. I think he was the one who smoked cigars, but who didn't have a corner office."

It was a Saturday. They phoned the judge at home and said they'd be over to talk. Outside the temperatures had reached all of seventeen degrees above zero. The thirty-degree rise in temperature did feel better. Turner doubted if it would reach the promised above freezing.

The judge lived in a condominium on the lake in Evanston. They drove up Lake Shore Drive to Sheridan Road, took the curve around the cemetery that bordered Chicago and Evanston, and turned right on the first street they could off of Sheridan in Evanston.

The judge greeted them at the door and smiled pleasantly. He offered them refreshments, which the detectives turned down.

Judge Wright smoked long thin cigars that smelled of rosewood. Turner enjoyed the aroma. The room they sat in had floor-to-ceiling bookcases. The volumes nearest Turner were fiction. The top shelf had what looked to him like a complete set of Dickens. The couch and matching chairs were brown corduroy. The furniture sat on a champagne-colored shag rug. In front of a stone fireplace was a desk that Turner guessed might have come from as far back as the American Revolution.

"How is the investigation going?" Wright asked.

"That's why we're here, your honor," Turner said. "We've been going through Judge Meade's decisions. The ones he wrote, and the ones he concurred with, and who he disagreed with."

"Yes?" The judge tapped cigar ash into a large glass ashtray in the shape of the United States.

"He wrote his own decisions, but we discovered that any controversial decisions, except the gay ones, were always written by you."

"And that means?"

"Why was that?"

"This has something to do with murder?"

"We're checking every aspect of his life."

"How efficient."

Turner asked, "Is there a reason for this sarcasm, your honor?"

He puffed on his cigar. "I've never actually seen Chicago's Finest at work."

"Are all the clerks and judges as snotty as the lawyers?" Fenwick asked.

The judge's reaction to this crack was to smile condescendingly and flip more ashes into his glass receptacle.

Turner said, "Why did he write only those opinions on gay people? They were as controversial as any others."

More cigar puffing. "Al Meade was a bright enough man. I was brighter. He had the courage of his convictions. He'd sign on, but he wouldn't write them. He never explained why he wanted to write the gay decisions. There have been only three since he's been on the bench. Either way, it gave both of us great satisfaction to see liberals squirm."

"Weren't you afraid of protests?"

"Judges make tough decisions. Somebody is always going to criticize. That never changes. Al had more controversy about him because he made a lot of public appearances. Some judges make speeches and some don't. He did. He was never going to be appointed to the Supreme Court unless right-wing conservatives took over Congress and the Presidency. His paper trail left no doubt where he stood on social issues."

"If you were so pleased to see liberals squirm, why didn't you have fights with Judge Malmsted, like Judge Meade did?"

"I like Judge Malmsted. I can sit down with her over a drink and discuss the fine points of legal decisions back to the days of Magna Carta. She is a brilliant woman. She is wrong most of the time, but if we based our relationships on who was right and who was wrong, would we ever get anywhere? We're civilized people."

"Except for whoever killed Judge Meade."

"With that exception."

"Francis Barlow, the clerk who worked in Judge Meade's office, said that Judge Wadsworth and Judge Meade had words the day of the decision on the Du Page County ruling."

"Which one was Barlow?"

"The supercilious, snotty one," Fenwick said.

"That's most of them."

Turner described him.

"Oh, yes," the judge said. "I remember him lurking around on occasion. Always had his nose in the air. My clerk spoke with me about him one time. He said Barlow was always rude to the other clerks, wouldn't help, and wouldn't go along. I believe I heard Al Meade chiding him one day about his attitude toward his fellow workers."

"Do you remember what he said?"

"No. It was something brief. As in any office, there are conflicts. I'm sure it was some such simple thing. I have no idea of any words Wadsworth and Meade may have had, or for that matter that Barlow and Meade may have had or even Barlow and Wadsworth."

"What was the most serious disagreement Meade had with Judge Malmsted?"

"Really, these were all civilized people. Federal judges have made hundreds of thousands, probably millions of decisions in this country. They don't kill each other."

"That's what Judge Wadsworth said."

"And I agree with him."

Fenwick said, "This is total bullshit."

Turner interrupted before Fenwick could get into a full-scale set-to with another judge who may or may not have friends with clout. Turner thought Fenwick was pushing his luck.

Turner said, "We need answers, your honor, and you haven't been cooperative. None of you have, really. We've got a homicide to solve."

"I find you both terribly amusing," Wright said. He managed to make a cough sound like a condescending put-down. He took a large silk handkerchief out of the pocket of his smoking jacket and brushed specks of dust from the clothes covering the mound of his corpulent belly. His movements and manner reminded Turner of a bishop in a movie set at the time of the French Revolution. The kind of bishop you'd hope the Revolutionist had gotten hold of early on and used for guillotine practice.

Wright said, "Sneer as you like, but we all really did get along better than most offices. Malmsted and Meade did fight often. Everybody knew it. I more than like Rosemary Malmsted. Our families are close. I've known her father for years. It is just an oddity that we're on opposite sides of the political spectrum, although your basic wealthy Republican is not all that different from your wealthy Democrat. Meade and Malmsted had words last week, before the Du Page County decision. She came to me to talk. She was furious. She has an uncle who is gay. I deflected her as much as possible, but she decided she was going after Al Meade with a vengeance. Al was never good at smoothing things out. He always knew the wrong thing to say. He was good at throwing gasoline on dying embers. I liked Al. He played a great round of golf. I went to sporting events with him. He just shot his mouth off once or twice too often. Maybe that's what killed him."

"You think Malmsted murdered him?" Turner asked.

"No, I didn't mean that. You asked for problems. I've just given you the biggest and the most obvious, and the one pertaining to your case."

"Anybody else hear them argue?" Turner asked.

"No, it was just outside my chambers. She'd asked to meet with us early before the decision came out. None of the office help were in. The three of us had talked and gotten nowhere. The two of them left and continued arguing just outside my door. I could hear them clearly."

"Why argue then? The decision must have long since been decided on and written."

"Judge Malmsted wanted to make her point. Making a point was something she felt she was good at."

Nothing further he added helped them with their case.

In the car Fenwick said, "They need to pass a new law. They can call it the Fenwick Is Pissed Act. Judge Wright is a perfect example. Whoever pisses me off gets arrested."

"Do you have to know them personally or can it just be on television or in a newspaper?"

"Either. I don't like these people."

"Me neither."

"Nothing clever or witty to say about them?"

"Don't like is don't like, what's to add?"

"Where to?"

"The Meade kid's hideaway is on our way back. Let's stop and see if he's in. If he's not there, we can try at his mom's. And we better talk to Malmsted again. She's the angry flash-point. We get no confirmation anywhere that Meade and Wadsworth didn't like each other, except from Barlow."

"I think we need to lean on Mr. Francis Barlow. He's got secrets to tell."

They devoured sandwiches at a small take-out deli on Howard Avenue.

As they drove up to Mike Meade's apartment, they saw a blue-and-white squad car parked in the alley next to the building. The driver's side door was open with a cop standing in the opening. His partner leaned against the back of the car. Both cops were staring up at the building.

Turner and Fenwick moseyed over.

They showed their identification.

"What's up?" Fenwick asked.

"Neighbor reported a window smashed a few minutes ago. Might have been a backfire in the alley or a gun shot immediately prior to the window being broken. Nobody answered our knock on the manager's door. The neighbor said it was in the apartment next to hers. She let us in the building. When we knocked on the door of the apartment, no one answered."

They followed the gaze of the uniformed cop to where a curtain was blowing out of a window.

"Is that Mike Meade's?" Turner asked.

"I hope not," Fenwick said.

They got the neighbor's name, walked over, and rang the bell. Turner said, "Police," into the intercom. She buzzed them in. If he were a crook, Turner would use the same method to get into any building.

On the third floor, they met the inquisitive tenant, a young woman named Elmira Wiggins. She said, "I was taking a shower. I thought I heard noise from next door and then the window smashed."

"Did it sound like a quarrel? People shouting?"

"No. More like somebody maybe bumping into things. Maybe throwing things. It's the middle of the day, and I had my stereo on loud. I was getting ready to go to work. The last noise, before the window, might have been a gun shot, or a car backfiring in the alley. After I was dressed, I tried knocking on his door, but nobody answered. There hasn't been any noise since the window broke."

They joined the beat cops out in the hall.

"We're going in," Turner said.

Everybody nodded.

"Allow me," Fenwick said.

He raised his foot to kick in the door.

"Stop!" Turner ordered.

They all looked at him.

"What happened the last time you did that, Buck?"

"Busted three bones in my foot."

"I'm not going to chance getting stuck with Carruthers while you recover." Turner asked the beat cops to try the manager again. As they turned to go, Fenwick tried the knob. It turned and the door swung open. Turner entered the room first.

They found Mike Meade dead under the small window in the bathroom.

19

As they stooped over the body, Fenwick said, "Double and triple fuck."

"Can't argue with that," Turner said.

The bullet had made a hole in the right side of Mike Meade's forehead. Blood and gore from the exit wound had splattered on the tiles in the shower. Blood covered the back of one hand. Turner guessed that the window was broken when his body was flung back with the force of the gun shot.

Turner and Fenwick carefully walked away from the body. They'd wait for the arrival of the Crime Lab and ME people before they did anything besides ascertaining that Meade was dead.

From the entry they observed the room. The couch was shoved up against the wall. Clothes from the closet were strewn about the room. The kitchen table was on its side. The lone chair was in the corner of the room nearest to the bathroom.

"Fight," Fenwick said.

"That's the thumping the neighbor heard?"

"She kill him?"

"Have to ask."

While they waited for the technicians to arrive, Turner and Fenwick interviewed the woman next door. Elmira Wiggins' apartment was as small as Meade's but with a great deal more furniture. Turner would have called it Victorian whorehouse, which he suspected may have been connected to her profession. The plush, pink pillows, the red lighting, the bright orange carpeting were as much a giveaway as her cut-to-the-crotch, skintight leather skirt only a hooker wore in weather like this.

Elmira was in her early twenties. She repeated her story. "He was never here that much. I only heard him once in a while. I met him in the hall several times. Once, I stopped over to discuss the way the management treats us. He seemed shy. I tried to be friendly, but he didn't respond."

Turner wondered if she'd made an offer that Meade could refuse.

In the hallway Turner said, "She is not high on my suspect list."

"Definitely not a keeper," Fenwick said. "Wonder if her name's really Elmira."

They joined the technicians in the apartment. One of the men from the Crime Lab and a woman from the ME's office stood with the two detectives in the middle of the room.

"Fight. Shot. Dead," was the guy from the Crime Lab's take on the matter.

"Sums it up," Fenwick said. "Let's go home."

"Need to check the wound," Turner said. "Match the bullet or what you can find of it, with what you've got from his dad."

"Already on it."

"Blood on the hand caused from when it hit the window."

"You're sure?"

"Glass in the cuts. Only glass that's broken is the window. Probably hit it after he got shot. Reflex. Body thrown back on impact."

Turner loved it when technicians confirmed his observations.

A uniformed cop came in. "Nobody else home on this floor. Nobody on the floor above or below heard anything. With the temperature up, lots of people are out getting groceries and stuff."

Just after they took the body away, the technicians left.

They returned to the bathroom. "Cool in here," Turner said.

"Broken windows in January will do that," Fenwick commented.

Turner touched the radiator. "Feels kind of cool."

Fenwick reached out to touch it.

"Wait," Turner said. He noted the spots where paint flecked off and dust was scattered on it. "Let's get the techs back in here. I want this examined. If they struggled, the killer might have brushed against this."

"Or touched it inadvertently," Fenwick suggested, "or simply brushed up against it."

The bathroom cabinet had a toothbrush, toothpaste, an electric razor, and a comb. The only drawers were the ones in the hallway, which doubled as a clothes closet. Turner and Fenwick opened them. One of them contained what would generously be called his outfits for dancing. Clean, neat, skimpy, and no clues to murder.

"These things all his?" Fenwick asked.

"Presumably." Turner held up a fishnet G-string. "I'd like to see Ben in something like this."

"Or Madge," Fenwick said.

They finished their brief inspection and returned to the main room.

"I get to ask the question of the hour," Fenwick said.

"I don't know," Turner said.

"I didn't ask."

"One killer or two? The question isn't much more obvious than the sunrise, and I don't know the answer. Thought I'd save you the energy."

"You're a pal."

"Let's get to Mrs. Meade. This is not going to be pleasant."

* * *

It was worse than they imagined. When they told Mrs. Meade, she collapsed on the floor and moaned. They helped her to a couch. Her daughter, Pam, entered the room.

She hurried to her mother. "What's wrong?" she asked.

Mrs. Meade continued moaning.

Pam turned to the cops. "What's happened?"

They told her.

Abruptly she sat on the edge of the couch. She continued to pat her mother's hand absently. "I don't believe it," she whispered.

"We're sorry," Turner said.

She nodded.

"We need to look in his room," Turner said.

She pointed to a hallway on the right. They eased out of the room and down the hall. The first door was a bathroom—the second a bedroom.

"Got to be his?" Fenwick asked.

Turner gazed at the four posters of male sports stars on the walls. Baseball, basketball, hockey, football. All Caucasian males. All with poses that emphasized their crotches. Mike Meade's parents weren't the only ones who missed the obvious.

They inspected the room carefully. Under the right side of the mattress, they found two male pornographic magazines with several pages in each stuck together.

"At least he was normal," Turner said.

"How's that?"

"He beat off."

Fenwick inspected the closet while Turner started on the desk.

"These all his?" Fenwick called.

"What?" Turner joined him.

Fenwick showed him the label on a pair of pants. "I've got size twenty-eight waist and thirty length on most of these, but I've got two with thirty-inch waists and thirty-four length."

"The change in waist I can see," Turner said, "not in length. Not that much."

"He had a boyfriend stay the night here?"

"I don't remember him mentioning any boyfriends."

"You don't remember it because he didn't mention it."

"I want to know more about Mr. Boyfriend. Why wasn't this stuff at his place in Rogers Park? Why here? It isn't the usual practice for severely closeted gay men to entertain their lovers in their parents' house, or for them to leave clothes behind."

"Maybe there's a logical, nonintimate explanation."

"I'm listening."

"I didn't say I had one. I just said there might be one."

Turner returned to the desk. He found paper clips, pens, pencils, blank notebooks, college papers, a bank book, and a package of glow-in-the-dark condoms.

"I didn't know they made these," Turner said.

"What?"

Turner showed him.

They found nothing else that led to either an explanation for why father and son should be dead or any lead to who the boyfriend might be.

"We've got to talk to the mother and daughter," Turner said. "Something is going on connected to them. They must know something."

Pam was at her mother's side. She was crying softly and holding her mother's hand.

Turner and Fenwick walked over to them.

"Please," Turner said, "if you could answer a few questions."

"I've phoned my mother's best friend. She'll be here any minute. My mom is not going to be able to talk. I don't know how I'm going to be able to talk."

Mrs. Meade stared straight ahead. Her blinks seemed to come minutes apart and seemed to take hours to complete. She responded with silence to questions. She did not move when touched. Turner suggested to Pam that she call the family doctor as well as the friend.

She spent several minutes making calls.

When the friend arrived, they managed to maneuver Mrs. Meade so she was lying down on the couch. They left them and moved to the next room.

When they were seated again Pam said, "I wish I could yell at you again, as I did the other day. I don't know why I'm not screaming myself into insensibility. I loved my brother. We were very close." She began to cry. A large number of tissues later, she was composed enough to speak.

"I don't know what I can tell you."

"Your brother claimed you knew he was gay," Turner said.

"Yes, he told me last summer. We have a cottage in the Upper Peninsula of Michigan. He and I were there for a week before our parents came up. We both brought boyfriends."

"Was he a lover or boyfriend or casual acquaintance?"

"More than a casual acquaintance, but maybe not a boyfriend. They slept in the same bed, but from what Mike said, I didn't think they were in love. They certainly had a good time together. This was a guy named Frank. He might have met him at dad's office."

"Francis Barlow?" Turner asked. "Tall, hair combed back and greased down." Tall and slender enough to be a thirty-inch waist, thirty-four-inch length.

"Yes. At first I thought he might be kind of standoffish, but he turned out to be great. We listened to old Anna Russell albums or played silly board games. We laughed and had a great time."

"Did you know about Mike's apartment in Rogers Park?"

"Mike had an apartment in Chicago?"

Mike Meade had obviously not told her everything.

"Yes. He wasn't living in Bloomington. Did he tell you he was a dancer at a strip bar, and maybe making extra money on the side with the customers?"

She looked genuinely bewildered. "Mike would never do anything like that. There would be too much danger in doing harm to dad's career, and to his own future, for him to do something that stupid."

"How did he and your father get along?"

She hesitated.

They waited. The hesitation told Turner almost enough.

"Now that they're both . . ." she stopped. "I wouldn't have told you this if it was just my dad. I would never implicate Mike. He wouldn't have killed our dad." She sighed. "They fought a lot."

She sniffed and dabbed at her eyes with a tissue. "They fought about politics mostly. I think a lot of Mike's anger came from his being unable to be open about his sexuality. It got worse the last year or so. I would never have said anything to either of my parents about Mike's sexuality without Mike's permission. Mike wanted very badly to come out to dad. His desire for his dad's approval was enormous. He spent his childhood trying to please him. I felt helpless. I'd do what I could to keep them apart here at home, which wasn't hard because Mike wasn't around that much. If other people were in the house, they were very civil to each other. I always seemed to have friends over. I could do other little things for Mike, like make sure he had a chance to be with his friend at the cabin. I've never seen Mike happier than that week last summer. He wanted to tell my dad about his sexuality this vacation, but with the Du Page County decision, it just didn't work out. They fought almost every time they saw each other."

Fenwick said, "Mike wanted his dad's approval, but they kept on fighting?"

"Is that so odd? It was Mike's way of saying he'd grown up. That he was an independent person. My father was a very strong personality."

They told her what Mike had said about him and his father's actions on New Year's Eve.

"I know nothing of this," she said. "Mike said nothing to me. Was he really a stripper?"

"Yes."

She shook her head. "Telling Mom all this is going to be hell."

The doctor arrived. After examining Mrs. Meade, he advised against sedating her. The friend agreed to stay as long as necessary.

Turner and Fenwick left. Light snow had begun to fall as they made their way to the car.

"Malmsted or Barlow?" Turner asked.

"Which one's closer?"

"I don't have the master list. Let's stop at Area Ten and get Barlow's address. We have to go through the Loop to get to Malmsted's anyway."

At Area Ten, the hallways were a bit less jammed. The warmer temperatures had allowed most of the locals to wander back to their inadequately heated homes or hovels. A much larger crowd of reporters had taken their place. Cameras from three local stations were present.

The blond cop who'd apologized, Jason O'Leary, said, "You've both got a meeting in the commander's office. The superintendent is in with him."

Turner and Fenwick trudged down the hall toward the commander's office in the rear of the building. Fenwick hummed the melody from the grand march from *Aida*.

"I'm the one who's supposed to know opera. Why are you humming that?"

"Some commercial was using it for a jingle—carpets or hemorrhoids or something. I like the tune. You don't like opera anyway, how do you know what that tune is?"

"My gay opera gene may be defective, but I know some of the basics. Dated an opera queen for two weeks once. I even attended one. At the end of two weeks, I disliked him more than I did the opera."

They knocked at the commander's door. Neither the acting commander nor the superintendent smiled at them as they entered.

Drew Molton introduced the superintendent then said, "We

need an update on the Meade case. I filled the superintendent in on everything up to when you left this morning. The son dying complicates everything. The media frenzy is going to be overwhelming."

They gave them everything they'd done that day. They included the difficulties with the judges.

"I had calls on that," the superintendent said. "One from Judge Wadsworth and one just before I left to come here from a Judge Wright. Neither of them has any pull in the city that I'm aware of, so count yourself lucky. Wadsworth was very angry. He thinks he's got clout. Good thing for you he's not a criminal judge. I got an odd call from the FBI. They don't like you either, but none of us likes them, so I don't care. I haven't been a detective in a while. I understand your style. I understand your reputation. I understand your results. If you can be more gentle, I'd recommend it. What I need you to do is catch me a criminal."

If they didn't, Turner figured they could be writing traffic tickets in Hegewisch for the rest of their careers.

"We're on our way to talk to Malmsted and Barlow."

"Have somebody bring the kid in," Molton said. "You can probably get Malmsted just as fast by going yourself. Getting the suburban cops to go out there and then sending somebody to get her is a pain in the ass. Just let them know you're coming."

"Always do," Fenwick said.

They got Barlow's address and gave it to several uniforms so they could pick him up.

"If he's not home, stay there until he arrives," Fenwick ordered.

20

Malmsted was in. They sat in the same room as yesterday.

"Mike Meade was murdered this afternoon."

She gasped. Her hands flew to her mouth.

"Where were you today?" Fenwick asked.

"You can't think I killed them."

"Where were you?"

"Here."

"Any witnesses to that?"

"My husband went to the hardware store for several hours this morning. He's fixing up part of the basement. We all know I hated the judge. Why would you think I killed the son? I may have met him once or twice at the most. I'm sure I wouldn't remember him if he passed me on the street."

"We believe the two murders are related," Fenwick said.

"Do you have proof of that?"

Fenwick said, "Two members of the same family happen to be shot by strangers who did not rob them? Doesn't rank high on my coincidence meter. What are the odds on that happening?"

"What are the odds of a killer murdering two people in the same family? I think you have to look to the family itself. I admit I quarreled with the judge. If everybody who quarrels with a co-worker is to be accused of murder, the line would stretch from here to the moon."

"According to what we learned," Turner said, "your quarrels with Al Meade were more than just disagreements with colleagues. You had words with him the day of the Du Page County decision."

"Judge Wright told you that."

Turner said, "Judge Malmsted, we expect as much cooperation from judges as we do regular people when working on a homicide. That means the truth as often and as soon as possible."

"I'm trying to be helpful."

"When we were here before, you said the judge was stupid, that he didn't write his own decisions."

"Yes."

"Our research doesn't back that up," Turner said.

"I don't care about your research. I know what's true. Have you read any of his decisions yourselves?"

"Yes," Turner said.

"What did you think?"

"I didn't agree with them, but they made sense. Nothing I couldn't understand. Of course, I wasn't reading obscure rules on federal land grants."

"You read the 'socially significant' decisions?"

"Only two so far, but our researcher says . . ."

"I don't care about your researcher. I know."

"Neither Judge Wadsworth nor Judge Wright agrees with you."

"Ask that clerk of his, Barlow. I had some conversations with him. The ones who really know what's going on are the clerks. Judges don't have a clue most of the time to what they're doing. They're politically connected lawyers who may or may not know the law."

"Barlow told you the judge didn't write his own decisions?"

"Yes."

"What if he was wrong?"

"What do you mean?"

"We talked to him. He was supercilious and snotty. Why would you believe him and not your colleagues?"

"All of them are supercilious and snotty. I guess we believe what we want to believe. Never in my presence did Meade follow a legal argument to its logical conclusion. He was an idiot."

"Was he an idiot?" Turner asked, "or was it that he disagreed with you, and you couldn't stand that? That made you nuts and you decided to get even."

"There is not one shred of evidence that I was in town New Year's Eve. I have my parents, my brother, and my husband to prove it. They were all here. I didn't leave the house."

"Would they all lie for you?" Fenwick asked.

"I would never ask them to, nor is there any reason to. I didn't kill him."

"Do you own a gun?"

"No. I don't permit them in the house."

In the car Fenwick said, "She's got witnesses. I hate it when they've got witnesses."

"Seemed to be a heck of a lot of meetings between these people the day of the Du Page County decision. What was going on? We've got Meade, Wright, Malmsted, and Wadsworth in various combinations."

"Maybe they met like that all the time."

"I bet not. We'll have to get copies of everybody's schedule. We can check Meade's at Area Ten." Which they did as soon as they arrived. Turner found the appointment book, and he and Fenwick perused it for several minutes. Some days the judges had numerous meetings, most often not.

"Number of meetings means shit," Fenwick said.

"I'm not sure," Turner said.

They were told that Francis Barlow had not been found. The beat cops had staked out his apartment. The calls to Barlow's friend in New York had gotten them a number no longer in service. Turner had a message to call Ian. He dialed his friend at the paper.

Ian said, "The Meade kid is dead?"

"Yep."

"Unbelievable. Who'd have it in for both father and son?"

"Gosh, golly, I don't know yet. When I find out, I'll be sure to call you first. Have you found anything recently?"

"I'm looking for a guy named Francis Barlow."

"Where'd you get that name?"

"From a list of people who worked in the office. He lives on the north side. If it's the same guy, Carl told me he'd been flirtatious a few times."

"I'm not surprised. Francis is gay."

"Flirtatiousness does not a faggot make."

"Sayings from Ian the wise. You could get a nine-hundred number and call it 'Ask Mr. Wisdom.' You think Carl was telling the truth? He was insightful enough to recognize he was being flirted with?"

"Probably. Maybe. I don't know."

"We have independent confirmation that Francis Barlow is gay. You have any leads on him?"

"I've been running a standard check through my grapevine. Up until recently at least, he had a membership in Body Beautiful, a gym down on Clark Street. My source thought he spent a good part of his Saturdays there. I was thinking of stopping by."

"Fenwick and I can check it out."

"You want this guy bad?"

"He may have been the boyfriend of Mike Meade."

"I want to go with you."

"No."

"Who's given you three major leads in this case?"

"I admit you've helped. How can I drag a reporter along? Acting Commander Molton has been terrific so far, and I don't want that to change. Besides, Barlow might not even be there."

"So then what have you lost if I come along?"

"No questions, no articles. If you're there, you're in the background. You are silent."

"I understand."
"Sorry."
"I was a cop. I do understand. I'm also a reporter. I shall be as discreet as you might wish."
"We'll pick you up," Turner said.
"Don't trust me to not run over there?"
"Ian, you are one of the best reporters around. I expect you would sell bushels full of relatives to get this story. You stay where you are. You've helped me, but I've also given you what we've told no one else."
"I'm not going to wreck it," Ian said.
Turner filled in Fenwick as they drove to the newspaper.
"Ian is not a suspect?" Fenwick asked as he raced through the streets.
"He's my best friend besides Ben. He didn't kill anybody."
Fenwick gave a neutral grunt.
Ian was waiting at the front door of the newspaper.
The gym was on Clark, a block south of Montrose on the west side of the street.
As they drove over, Turner gave Ian more details on what they'd found out.
Fenwick added when he was done, "What I have a tough time with is this closeted stuff. Maybe it's because I'm straight. I understand a lot from being friends with you guys, but I don't know. That's a powerful lot of fear."
"I feel sorry for them," Turner said. "I know what it's like to be scared."
Ian said, "I don't see what the big problem is. I don't see why these people are so closeted. Twenty years ago, yes, but not today."
"Lots of gay people are still scared," Turner said.
"You have no need to be. No person in the city needs to be. Chicago has a nondiscrimination ordinance. You couldn't be fired. I think you should join that gay cop organization. In fact, you'd be good at leading it."
"People are scared and have good reasons to be. You know

better than that. Discrimination these days is often more subtle where it can't be blatant. Personal slights, promotions skipped, missed opportunities, fear of personal attack. Being fired is the most obvious, but being antigay can take many forms."

Ian said, "The world has changed. You can't call us faggots on the floor of Congress without a storm of protest. Unless you're a religious nut and have your own call-in show, you can't be that vile. Of course, if you've got your own venue, you can say all the vicious lies you want about us, but who does that affect really? All this closeted stuff doesn't seem real to me. It just doesn't make sense."

Turner remembered the crack Ian had made the other day about closeted gay people. This latest was too much. He blew up at his friend. "Who the hell are you to talk about other people's closets? You work in an environment where being openly gay is never a problem. How pleasant and comfortable for you. How many gay people have that kind of luxury? Not very goddamn many. It's the gay reporters and journalists who are so goddamn holier than thou about the rest of us coming out, but they sit there in their safe little environments and judge the rest of us. How terribly brave for some fucking activist to tell me how to run my life."

Ian said, "The more of us who come out, the sooner we will have our rights."

"I've heard that a million times," Turner said. "Most of the time I think it's true, but people's fears and the knowledge that human beings can be massively cruel to one another is also true."

Ian said, "I wouldn't live in fear."

"How can you be so blind and unsympathetic to the compromises most of us have to make? Like you never made alterations to hide your sexuality. We were lovers, Ian. I know you. We've all done the subtle little things to protect ourselves. The leaving out of information when having conversations with new people. The ingrained sense of self-preservation that keeps most of us from walking hand-in-hand down the streets of most cities, and in those few cities where we can, only in certain neighborhoods and often only in gay pride parades. We'd all like to be as out as you. Do you deny the dangers for some? Outside Chicago and a few rare suburbs, schoolteachers in this state can be fired if they're gay. Do you want them to announce their sexuality on television? Will you guarantee them a job if they get fired? Will you pay their rent? We're all being more out all of the time. Do you deny the dangers for some? Even you, Ian, would hesitate to walk hand-in-hand with another guy in Wicker Park and most of the other neighborhoods of this city that don't border on the lake. I don't blame anybody in the case we're investigating. I think they all have serious problems which I have sympathy for."

"Which have probably led to murder."

"We'll have to see about that."

Silence descended on the interior of the vehicle for the rest of the ride over. When they arrived outside the gym, Fenwick turned off the car. They sat quietly for several moments.

Fenwick said, "Can you guys work out this gay political shit later. I'm not trying to be insensitive here, but it's awful goddamn cold. I'd like to get started."

Ian spoke first. "I'm sorry," he said. "I forget sometimes. I know it's not easy. Sorry."

Turner drew a deep breath. "I shouldn't have blown up at you."

"Great, you made up nice," Fenwick said. "If you're going to kiss as well as make up, do it on your own time. You ready?"

"Let's get this guy," Turner said.

21

They entered the gym. At the reception desk, Turner and Fenwick showed their identification to a sweatsuit-clad twenty-year-old. She called the manager who accompanied them as they hunted for Barlow.

The health club was set up on three levels. The ground floor had row after row of exercise machines. The second floor was completely open for large exercise classes. The top floor contained a running track. Inside the oval was gymnastics equipment. Most gyms on the near-north side of the city had a large gay clientele. As far as Turner could see, that was true of this one as well.

They found Francis Barlow using a universal weight machine designed to increase his upper-arm strength. His plain gray T-shirt was cut off to expose his midriff. The cotton was damp down the front and at the armpits. Matted hair peeked out from around the collar of the shirt and glistened around his lower torso. His tight shorts bulged in the front, were damp at the crotch, and ripped up the sides. Turner could see the straps of a jock showing. The skimpy clothes showed off his taut muscled frame. His shoes were pure white, as were his socks. Every strand of his slicked-back hair was still in place. Sweat beaded on his upper lip and his forehead.

They stood directly in front of Barlow who stared at them as he finished his repetitions.

“I can’t stop my workout,” he said.

“Indeed, you can,” Fenwick said.

Barlow tried to stand up. Fenwick placed a large hand on the front of his T-shirt and shoved. Barlow sat back down. He picked up a towel from the floor and mopped at some of his sweat.

People around them were beginning to stare.

“What is it that you want?” Barlow asked.

“You were Mike Meade’s boyfriend,” Turner said.

“If I was, that is not a crime.”

“His death is.”

Barlow looked each of them in the eye. “That’s bullshit. What do you mean he’s dead? I saw him myself last night.”

The three men were silent.

Barlow turned pale. “No, that can’t be true.”

“He died this afternoon.”

“What happened?”

“That’s what we want you to tell us,” Turner said.

“I had nothing to do with his death.”

“We need for you to accompany us down to the station,” Fenwick said.

“Am I under arrest?”

“No.”

“Then why should I go down to the station?”

“We’re making the rules here, Mr. Barlow,” Fenwick said. “Cut the crap.”

Barlow said, “I would like to shower. I would prefer to be talked to in a less public place, but unless I’m under arrest, I don’t believe I have to accompany you anywhere. We can talk here. I need to take a shower first. This is horrible news about Mike. How can he be dead?”

Fenwick said. “We’ll accompany you to your locker.”

“You a closet case?” Barlow asked.

“Not this week,” Fenwick said.

The three men stood at the opening to the shower room as Barlow ran spray over himself. The two cops were not about to risk another possible witness getting away. The other patrons, seeing three fully clad men watching Barlow, either grinned lasciviously or frowned worriedly and hurried out. Turner didn't find himself the least excited by what he saw.

Barlow took his time in his ablutions. Turner noted Fenwick getting testy. Fenwick didn't look like he'd be the slightest bit gentle with this man.

The club permitted them to sit in an unused office to ask their questions. Barlow wore a black Air Apache Flight Suit. He sat rigidly in the office chair and crossed his legs at the ankles just above his black Georgian Logger boots. He rested an elbow on the desk. His hair was now genuinely wet while being slicked back.

Turner sat on the desk near to Barlow. Fenwick and Hume stood against opposite walls.

"Tell me what happened," Barlow said.

Turner noted that Barlow's hands trembled slightly. One foot tapped the other regularly. Barlow's rigid control was cracking.

"When was the last time you saw Mike Meade?"

"He called me last night from his house after you were through with him. I stopped over. I didn't ring the bell. I waited in my car outside. Reporters were lurking all over the place. When I got there, he ran out and jumped in the car. He was angry about what you had accused him of. The poor guy was a mess. He felt really guilty about his dad."

"You mean he killed him?" Fenwick asked.

"No, not that. About the things he said to him before he died. He was heartbroken. He really loved his dad. He wanted to talk. We went to his place in Rogers Park. He cried a lot. We spoke until about four this morning. I left. He stayed there."

"Do you have proof that you went home?"

"I have proof for none of this. At the time I went home, the streets were quite deserted. I saw no one. I slept until nearly one this afternoon. I went out and ate at a health food restaurant near my home. Then I came here, and I've been here ever since."

"Tell us about your relationship with Mike Meade."

"We were good friends, but we were never lovers."

"His sister told us you spent a week with him at their cabin. We found pants in his closet that are likely your size. You were more than friends."

"I must have left the pants in the cabin by accident."

"Tell us about you and him," Turner said.

"First, you tell me what happened to him. You say he's dead." Barlow's voice wavered. Turner saw the pursed lips loosen and tremble. Barlow leaned over, put his elbows on his thighs, and intertwined his fingers. He looked up at Turner. "Please tell me what happened."

"You wanted to be lovers, but he didn't," Turner said.

Barlow looked at the ground. Turner saw Barlow nod his head as he whispered, "Yes." Turner saw a tear fall to the ground. Turner and Fenwick were masters at waiting for a suspect to speak. After a few minutes Barlow wiped his nose on his expensive sleeve and began. "We met at the bar Au Naturel. I knew who he was, though. I'd seen him from a distance at the office once. At the bar it was his night off, and he was by himself having a beer. I introduced myself to him, mentioned I saw him at the office. He became quite concerned. I assured him my interest was in him and how good-looking I thought he was, not in any connection with his dad. That was true. I didn't date him because it could help my career. How could it? I liked him because he lived a looser, unstructured life. Mine is pretty rigid."

"Did he talk to you about coming out to his parents?"

"He was never out to his dad or mom. As far as I knew, he'd told only his sister."

"Does your family know about you?" Turner asked.

"That I'm gay? No. That's why I took the job here. If I'd have gotten an offer from the West Coast, I'd have taken it. I needed to have some space. Mike and I shared that in common. It was good to have somebody to talk to who wasn't judgmental. Guys I'd date a few times were always asking about why I didn't come out to my parents. One guy wanted me to go with him to a party with his co-workers on that National Coming Out Day last October. I broke up with him because of that. I'll come out in my own good time."

"What happened with you and Mike?"

"We began dating. It was amusing in the office. The judge would be bragging about his kid, but I was the one who knew the true story."

"When did you meet?"

"Last spring."

"And you were dating until now?"

"No. We dated for about three months, but he had odd hours and I have a great deal of work I bring home. We couldn't see each other that often. I wasn't about to go to the bar to get a feel, not when I'd been with him in bed."

"You broke up."

"I wouldn't put it like that. I told him I loved him. He said he wanted to just be friends, and we were good friends still. We could open up with each other without the demands of a lover's relationship. You probably wouldn't understand, but we were an outlet for each other."

"Fuck buddies," Fenwick said.

"Crudely put, yes, but not so much recently."

"But you each saw other people?" Turner asked.

"He did. I was too busy. Sometimes we'd get together and talk about who he was dating."

"That must have been difficult for you."

"Why?"

"Guy you loved telling about his dates."

"Hold it, you're getting this wrong. This isn't some jealous lover's murder here. If it was, why would I murder Judge Meade? I'd have been angry at Mike. We didn't have an angry breakup. That vacation last summer was the best time I've ever had."

"You knew he hustled?"

"Of course."

"That didn't bother you?"

"If we'd become lovers, it would have, but we weren't."

"Did you go skiing with him in Aspen this past week?" Turner asked.

Barlow hesitated.

"He told us he was with a wealthy client and then later with a friend. We can check the airlines. They'll have records. We can check your credit card company."

"I know that. We agreed to meet in Aspen after he was done with the client. I went with him to St. Louis. At each stop, he insisted that we stay in a room with two beds. He told me I could meet him as long as we got separate beds. We couldn't afford separate rooms. I admit, I would still have been happy to make love to him. What he didn't know about what I caressed while he slept wasn't going to hurt him."

"What did you do in St. Louis?"

"Tourist stuff. Went to the Arch, the train station, had dinner at Tony's restaurant."

"Fabulous place," Ian said.

"Yes, it is. Refined, elegant, and very expensive. As you know, the flight back to Chicago was delayed."

"What happened when you got here?"

"They gave us free drinks on the plane while it was delayed. We were feeling no pain. We walked off the plane arm in arm. His dad must have seen us. Mike gave me his baggage claim ticket so I could pick up his luggage and bring it to his place later. Mike was afraid he was going to be late for work, plus he said he had to meet somebody at the airport."

"Do you know who?"

"No."

"A client?"

"When he didn't give me a name or tell me it was a friend, I assumed it was a client. He never said."

"Then what happened?"

"He said he would find his friend and get a ride with him or take a cab with him. I wanted to go straight home. I had to get moving. I was supposed to meet my friend from New York for dinner, and I was very late myself. We said good-bye on the lower concourse. We were still pretty intoxicated, laughing and giggling. I teased him about the sugar daddy he was probably meeting. We were feeling really giddy. I grabbed him and kissed him good-bye. I figured, who would know me at the airport?"

"The judge saw you?" Turner asked.

"He came running up to us. He started berating Mike, calling him names, making cracks about him being a faggot, how dare he make a public display of affection—that kind of thing. I felt bad because it was my fault we kissed. I was feeling affectionate and New-Year's-party-happy. All the time he was castigating Mike, Judge Meade never raised his voice. Nobody around noticed us. Mike was really pale. Trembling. His dad looked like he was ready to hit him. I tried to get in between them. The judge turned on me. He told me he'd be sure I was fired as soon as he got back from Montreal. He said ordinance or no ordinance in the city of Chicago, he was going to find a way to fire me. He said that it applied only to city workers, not to federal employees."

"Is that true?" Fenwick asked.

"I think so," Ian said.

"I was willing to stay, but Mike said I better go. His dad told me to get the hell out. I began walking away. Mike ran up to me a minute later and said everything would be all right. He'd take care of my job and not to worry about his dad. From all I knew of Judge Meade, I didn't have much faith in Mike's reassurance. I assumed my job was gone. I got in the cab and went to meet my friend. We went out to dinner as I stated earlier."

"We haven't been able to get hold of your friend."

"Barry has trouble with the phone company periodically. You'll get hold of him. He'll back up what I say."

"Why didn't you tell us about you and Mike Meade when we talked to you earlier?"

"You didn't ask. I hadn't had a chance to talk to Mike. Since I knew he'd seen his dad, I didn't want to implicate him."

"Or yourself," Turner said.

"I didn't find out about the murder until that Friday morning when I came in to work. New Year's Day I was skiing just over the border in Wisconsin. I don't listen to the news."

They left Barlow in the room and met outside.

Fenwick said, "Jealous old lover, about to lose his job. He has all the makings of a fine suspect."

"Sort of fits," Turner said, "I'm just not sure, although he's going to have to come down to the station. We'll have to question him again."

"Who could Mike Meade have been going to meet that night?" Ian asked.

"If he was really meeting someone," Fenwick said. "Making that up would be something good to add if Barlow needed an out."

Turner said, "Why would Mike or Judge Meade need to go to the Federal Building? What makes that place so important?"

"I hate coincidences," Fenwick said.

"So it's important?"

Fenwick shrugged. "Apparently so."

Turner continued, "If what Schurz told us is true, both of them went there. Mike didn't have to meet his dad. He was already with his dad. If he left his dad, how did the judge know to go to the bar. Did the kid leave and Judge Meade begins to follow his kid all over town? Is this making sense?"

"We weren't there," Fenwick said. "We don't know what was going on."

"Got to be a logical progression," Turner said. "The judge

and the kid are at the curb at the airport fighting. Kid claimed his dad must have followed him secretly."

"Mike Meade said they didn't meet, but that his dad followed him at a distance," Fenwick said.

Ian said, "He lied."

"We have corroboration from Barlow about the fact that dad and son met," Turner said. "I just can't get them from the airport to Au Naturel."

"How long is it between sets at the bar?" Fenwick said.

"Forty-five minutes to an hour," Ian answered.

Fenwick said, "That's plenty of time to leave, commit murder, and get back. Maybe he met his dad afterward. What if Schurz got the times confused and saw him much later than he said? Maybe the conversation didn't end in the bar. Schurz could remember things backward. Maybe he wanted to impress you."

"The kid was whacked," Turner said, "but I don't think he'd get it that wrong. He was a needy, frightened teenager, but he wasn't stupid."

Ian said, "He had a little bit of information and to get closer to you, maybe trying to impress you, he gave you more than he had. He wanted to be important. He wanted to be needed. If he knew something important, then he was important."

"We're getting awfully speculative here," Fenwick said. "I like the idea that Mike Meade left the bar between sets."

"For an assignation in the Federal Building?" Ian asked.

"We have no corroboration that he was there," Turner said.

"Discount all of what Schurz had and what do we have?" Ian asked.

"Barlow and the mysterious stranger Mike Meade was meeting at the airport," Fenwick replied.

"Which at least helps Barlow," Turner said. "We still haven't talked to his alibi. And he could have gone out afterward. Killed the judge. His lover is in pain. Hell, he and Mike Meade could have killed his dad, and Mike Meade feels such guilt that he's going to turn them both in."

"The son has to die to ensure silence?" Fenwick asked.

The door to the office opened.

"Can I leave?" Barlow asked.

"We need to bring you down to the station," Turner said. "We're going to have to do more checking."

Barlow nodded. "Let me get my stuff."

Fenwick accompanied him to the locker room.

Ian said, "I don't trust Barlow."

"We don't have any physical evidence that he is the killer. I don't like it that the only people who can contradict his story are dead."

Ian said, "I'm going back to the office. I'm going to try squeezing my sources some more. Barlow must have friends in the gay community. I'm going to find them. And you don't have to remind me. None of this is publishable. But I expect a complete, utter, and entire exclusive on this."

"Would you settle for a hot date with an NFL quarterback?"

"As long as he's under thirty, sure."

Ian left.

As Turner and Fenwick took Barlow back to the station, light snow drifted in a diminishing wind. As they crossed the Chicago River on Lake Shore Drive, Turner looked west to the towers of light shrouded in cold. The snow made them even more stark and beautiful than usual.

22

At Headquarters, they put Barlow in one of the conference rooms. They informed Molton of what they had.

The acting commander said, "We have something here?"

"My instinct is against arresting him," Turner said.

"Let's keep him talking for a while," Fenwick said. "He's a great suspect, but I agree with Paul. We don't have anything physical to tie him to either killing. Tough to make that stick in court."

Molton nodded agreement.

By ten o'clock, Turner was sick of going over the same questions with Barlow. The suspect was exhausted and frightened, but showed no signs of knowing more than he said. Turner thought one good thing was that at least the guy had dropped most of his arrogance.

Turner and Fenwick took a break from the conversation. They sat at their desks. Turner called Ben to tell him he would be very late and not to wait up.

After Turner hung up, Fenwick said, "What I really need is chocolate."

"Fresh out."

"Never be too far from your nearest supply of chocolate. One of the great truisms of the twentieth century. I want it on my headstone in huge block letters." Fenwick opened every drawer of his desk and moved everything around. He came up with nothing.

"Preliminary lab reports on Mike Meade's apartment are here," Turner said. He glanced through them.

"Anything?"

Turner read for a few moments. "Nope. No prints on the radiator although a couple of dust smudges could be fresh. A few paint flakes might be newly broken."

"I can see it now," Fenwick said. "We line up the suspects and look for microscopic bits."

"If we find the killer, it could be a damning piece of evidence."

"The kind of thing that is dear to my heart. Not as dear as chocolate, but right up there."

Turner asked, "Where are the reports we wrote on our first conversation with Barlow?"

Fenwick pointed to a stack of papers on the floor next to his desk.

Turner grabbed the pile and put it on top of his desk.

"Let's go over the first stuff he said," Turner suggested. He found the appropriate pages. He walked down to the second floor, made a copy, and brought them back up.

He and Fenwick read through what they had written.

Turner said, "Only big oddity is that stuff about Wadsworth and Meade having arguments. Absolutely nobody confirmed that."

"I assumed he was lying."

"Let's try it the other way around," Turner said. "Let's assume that everything Barlow said was true. Remember he never actually lied to us the first time, he just left stuff out."

"Lots of important stuff."

"I agree, but we're stuck. Let's try Barlow as personification of truth."

"You're cute when you use six syllable words."

"Why don't you sit on it and rotate. I'm even cuter when I

solve a murder. From Barlow, we believe that Wadsworth and Meade were mortal enemies."

"We are not going to be able to pin a murder rap on Judge Wadsworth based on what we've got so far."

"Let's talk to Barlow some more. If necessary, let's get Wadsworth down here."

"Based on this?"

"Hell, you were ready to arrest Judge Wright on little more than this."

"Yeah, but I get to be the impulsive one in this relationship. That's my job."

"Yeah, well, get used to it. Let's try Barlow again."

When they entered the room, Barlow was sitting with his elbows on the table, rubbing his eyes with his fists."

He looked at them. He said, "I'm scared."

"Of what?" Turner asked.

"That you're going to try to hang this on me. If nothing else, even if I'm associated with this, my career will be ruined. You guys don't understand what it's like being gay and trying to get a job and having to lie."

"I understand," Turner said. "I'm gay."

Barlow searched his eyes. "Are you telling me the truth or is that a lie to get me to have confidence in you?"

"I'm not going to shove my tongue down your throat to prove it. I have a lover named Ben. He is a kind, strong, good man. He is at home right now. I would prefer to be in bed with him than here with you."

"Okay."

Fenwick said, "We've been going over what you told us the first time. We're curious about this statement about Judges Wadsworth and Meade arguing."

"I know what I saw and heard."

"Was it just that one time? Maybe he'd met someone in the hall on his way back from the meeting."

"I was in the corridor waiting to meet with him. I heard them and afterward as we walked down the hall Judge Meade kept muttering under his breath about Judge Wadsworth."

"What did he say exactly?"

"Just muttered. All I heard were Wadsworth and Malmsted's names. She and Judge Meade had words earlier that day."

"Meade and Malmsted fought a lot."

"Yes. Mostly it was all very civil, at least what I saw. They'd talk to each through gritted teeth. They'd take out their disagreements in court sometimes. If a lawyer was arguing the liberal side of a case, Meade would ask him all kinds of tough, arrogant questions designed more to harass the lawyer than for any judicial purpose. When it was the other side's turn, Malmsted would start in on that lawyer. It's all very polite and proper, mostly, but you could tell they were going after each other."

"And Wadsworth and Meade fought at other times?"

"Three times. Twice before the Du Page County decision and once three days before New Year's Eve. The day before I left for Aspen to meet his son, Judge Meade told me I was supposed to call the judicial misconduct board. He told me to find the number and who you were supposed to talk to. He also wanted me to research something called a 'good behavior clause.' "

"What's that?"

"Federal appellate judges are constitutionally protected. They can be impeached, but it's only happened a few times. I didn't have time to look up the 'good behavior' materials. I presume it has something to do with firing somebody for moral turpitude, although all the judges could get together and recommend another judge be fired. I don't know how that works."

"What if it wasn't Malmsted?" Turner said.

"Huh?" Barlow said.

"Did he actually give you the name of the judge he was talking about?"

"No. I never asked. I found out the information and put it on his desk. It was just a name and phone number."

Turner motioned to Fenwick. They left the room.

Turner said, "For all his supposed surface politeness, Meade was doing an awful lot behind the scenes. Lots of angry meetings, although we have mostly Barlow's word for this. Meade's better at hiding his frustration and anger than the others, but it gets to be too much. He explodes at Wadsworth."

"Then he shoots Wadsworth, because the judge is evil. Let's go arrest Meade. He did it."

"I hate it when you're sarcastic."

"The wrong guy's dead according to your theory. We could shoot Wadsworth and make it even."

"I wonder if Malmsted knew about fights between Meade and Wadsworth," Turner said.

"We've been leaning on Barlow, we could pressure her a little."

Turner glanced at his watch. "Little late for calling."

"Just before midnight on a cold winter's night, sounds like a great beginning for a poem," Fenwick said.

"You are not to start quoting poetry," Turner said.

"Doing my best." Fenwick reached for the phone. "It's a murder investigation. I like shaking up suspects."

While Fenwick talked, Turner read through more lab reports.

After Fenwick hung up he said, "Judge Malmsted is not a happy camper."

"*How to Win Friends and Influence Suspects* by Buck Fenwick."

"Has a nice ring to it," Fenwick said. "She was up reading. Malmsted said she knew nothing about fights between those two. She did remember one time this week, when she heard Meade telling Wadsworth he needed to talk to him about his kid."

"He said this in front of her?"

"She remembered it as an off-hand comment, she said Meade sounded almost sarcastic. She passed it off as him being mean or stupid. She couldn't remember which day this was. I asked her if she could recall anything else they said to each other that might be significant. That's all she could come up with."

"Wadsworth versus Meade," Turner said. "He told us everybody got along, but they didn't. He was one of the one's who hasn't been honest with us. I want to talk to his eminence."

"No calls. Let's go visit him. Maybe we'll wake him up. I've always wanted to wake up a judge. This should be lots of fun. Making judges miserable could become a habit."

"What do we do with Barlow?"

"Keep him here. I want to know exactly where he is."

They drove to Judge Wadsworth's home. Fenwick pulled into the circular drive in front of the fifty-story condominium complex. Flakes of snow drifted in occasionally off the lake. They showed their identification and told the doorman who they wanted to see.

A woman in her early fifties in a drab gray sweatsuit answered the door.

They showed her their identification. She said she was Mrs. Wadsworth.

"We're looking for your husband," Turner said.

"He's not here," she said.

"Where could we find him?" Turner asked.

She gave them a puzzled look. "What is this about?"

"We're investigating the murders of Judge Meade and his son," Fenwick said. "We need to talk to him about where he was early today."

"He went out this morning for the paper and some groceries."

"Where was he on New Years Eve?" Fenwick asked.

"I'm sure he told you. We went out to dinner. We came back here and went to bed."

"He didn't get up and go anywhere?"

"I wouldn't know. We have separate bedrooms. He snores. Will you leave us alone?"

"Where is he?"

She hesitated and finally shrugged. "He left for his office half an hour ago."

They drove to the Kennedy Federal Building. Fenwick has ceased grumbling about the cold. They found Wadsworth standing behind his desk. He was wearing a camel's-hair coat open over a white sweater and jeans. He did not invite them in or ask them to sit.

"Gentlemen, this better be good. It is the middle of the night. I will be on the phone to your superiors as soon as you leave, no matter what it is you've come to speak to me about. Furthermore, I spoke earlier with Judge Wright and Judge Malmsted. They were not positive about either of you. We may be collectively filing a complaint."

Turner said, "You were the judge that Meade was going to try and get fired. It wasn't Malmsted he wanted to haul before a judicial review board. Why was he going to turn you in?"

"I don't know what you're talking about."

"He was going to turn someone in. Everybody figured it was Malmsted, but it was you."

"You've been talking to Barlow again? He doesn't know anything."

Turner said, "We need to go over where you were on New Year's Eve and where you were all this morning."

"I was home all day today."

"Oops, mistake," Fenwick said, "Your wife said you went out for the paper and some groceries. Where were you this morning, Judge Wadsworth?"

"I got the groceries and came back."

"We'll need to see the receipts."

"This is absurd. This conversation is over. You're both leaving."

"No," Fenwick said. He leaned his bulk casually against the door as if neither he nor it were planning to move before the next ice age rearranged the Midwest.

"You'll both lose your jobs for this."
"Is that all you judges ever say?" Fenwick said. "It's boring."
"We're going to talk," Turner said. "Where were you New Year's Eve?"
"Home."
"Why are you here now?" Fenwick asked.
"I had to get some work done."
"At midnight?" Fenwick asked.
"People work late as your presence here attests."
"With your coat on?" Fenwick asked.
"You're being absurd."
"Speaking of your coat. We may need that," Fenwick said.
"What on earth for?"
"Microscopic check. The killer banged against something in Mike Meade's apartment. Traces will be on the killer's clothing."
The judge's right hand began to reach for his coat sleeve, then stopped.
Turner and Fenwick noted the movement.
"We need a search warrant," Fenwick said, "One of us is staying around until it gets here."
"You're not going to find a gun," Wadsworth said.
Fenwick said, "We're going to get a microscopist to go over your clothes and your car for traces of Judge Meade's blood. We'll check fibers from your coat against those found in Mike Meade's apartment."
"This is an outrage."
"Maybe we don't need a warrant," Fenwick said. "We're already in."
Turner said, "We're not screwing this up. We need to call Area Ten and get Molton down here. This is going to be taken care of tonight."
Fenwick glared at the judge. "Your honor, you need to carefully take your coat off. Don't try and brush any part of it. Don't touch anything in this room. If you do either of those

things, I will cuff you immediately and we will continue this discussion down at Area Ten."

"How dare you."

"I can pull my gun and make this really dramatic," Fenwick said, "or you can do as I said very slowly and very carefully."

The judge complied with ill grace. Turner thought he saw him trying to snatch glimpses of the back and sleeves of the coat.

The standoff continued in the vestibule of the building for the hour it took for the calls to Area Ten, for Wadsworth's protests to be ignored, and for Molton to show up, search warrant in hand.

"You got it?" Fenwick said.

"I backed you guys as much as I could. Went out on a limb with a judge I know who hates federal judges. I think you might have something."

Turner and Fenwick hunted carefully through the entire office. At intervals they could hear the judge loudly protesting in the hallway. His calm demeanor was gone. The loudest protests came when his coat was taken away by the lab technicians. At three in the morning Turner began methodically going through the judge's Rolodex. In it they found several numbers listed under Lance Thrust's name. Mike was penciled in at the bottom of the entry. They dialed each of them. On one they got the answering machine in Bloomington. Another got them the bar. They got no answer when they called the third. Judge Wadsworth refused to tell them what it was. It took several calls to Headquarters, but the detectives eventually ascertained that it was the number to Mike Meade's cellular phone.

"Why do you have Mike Meade's unlisted cellular phone number in your Rolodex?" Turner asked.

"His father gave it to me."

"He never gave it to his father. His father didn't know he lived here and not in Bloomington."

Fenwick asked, "What's this nine-hundred number with no name next to it?"

"I don't remember."

Fenwick tapped in the numbers and listened to the receiver.

A few seconds later he held it out so they could hear. It was a recorded message asking for the caller's credit card number so they could begin having a party.

"Phone sex," Fenwick said. He listened another minute. "Male-to-male phone sex."

Wadsworth slumped onto his chair. He said, "You wouldn't understand."

"Try us," Fenwick said.

"You don't know what it is like being married and being gay. For years I kept myself under control. Relations with my wife were never great, but they were something. As we got older, they tapered off. We got separate rooms, which was good for both of us. I wasn't that interested any more. I began to go to a few bars. Then I went to that bar Au Naturel. I found one of the dancers attractive. I brought him to a hotel once in a while. I used a fake name. I had met Judge Meade's wife on occasion, but never his kids. I had my own courtroom. The picture of them on his desk is from when they were little. I found myself falling in love with Lance Thrust. To my surprise he returned my affection. I saw him at least once a week. I no longer had to go to the bar. I teased him about his name a lot. He wouldn't tell me his real name."

"Did he know who you were?"

"I don't think he did. Not until the last couple days for sure."

"How'd you find out his real name?"

"Late this summer, out of idle curiosity when he was in the shower, I looked in his wallet. I was stunned to realize it was Mike Meade. I did not confront him. I didn't know what to do. Al Meade was so smug about his antigay decisions. He made me furious, but I couldn't say much or he might become suspicious of my sexuality. He was trying to deny gay people their rights, when I was a better judge than he was, smarter, wrote better decisions, was more well-connected. I could barely contain myself. By early December I was convinced that I was in love with Mike Meade. Maybe he really was returning my affection, or maybe I'd deluded myself. I wouldn't be the first person on the planet to fall hopelessly in love with a whore. I didn't tell him what I knew. I kept the relationship going. I tried to do everything I could to make him love me back. Maybe partly it was for revenge on his dad, but I also really loved him."

Fenwick said, "He was an expensive whore. He wasn't in love with you. He certainly wasn't being faithful."

"I knew he went with other men, but I blotted that out of my mind. Love and revenge got mixed up. Meade kept pushing his homophobic views, and then with the Du Page County decision, I lost it. A couple days before New Year's, I blurted out that his son was gay.

"He wanted to know how I knew. On that day, I refused to tell him. I tried to get hold of Mike, but I couldn't. I don't think Judge Meade could either. Al Meade and I had an angry meeting first thing in the morning on New Year's Eve. God forgive me, I told him everything. He was furious. He said he was going to bring me up in front of the judicial commission. I found that amusing. His son was certainly of age."

"What happened later?"

"I was supposed to meet Mike at the airport. We planned this long before he left. We did talk briefly early that afternoon on the phone. I didn't want to tell him what I'd done until I saw him in person. I had to talk to him before his dad got to him. I offered to pick him up at the airport. I was going to tell him everything. We could talk at the Federal Building. I know ways to circumvent the security system. I felt terrible about not telling him about my fight with his dad, but I figured I'd be seeing him in a couple of hours. I came home with my wife and retired. As you know, we have separate rooms. This condominium is huge. It wasn't difficult to leave without her knowing.

"Mike told me later that his dad had seen him with his friend at the airport. He accused his son of being gay. Mike denied it and said he didn't know why I would say such things.

"They'd just separated when I found him. I gave Mike a big hug. His dad saw us together. For some reason he didn't confront us there, but he followed us to the Federal Building. We used the reserved entrance. Later, I would have to make sure the camera wasn't working, but it malfunctioned without my intervention.

"Mike and his dad were both like maniacs. Mike spilled out everything. About the sex we'd been having, about dancing in the bar."

Turner said, "Mike told us that his father didn't approach him at the airport."

"He was trying to protect me. He didn't know I killed his dad.

"Father and son were screaming and ranting at each other. Then Mike ran off. Al turned on me. I thought he would have a stroke on the spot. He made all kinds of threats. He was going to reveal my sexuality. He had to be stopped. He told me he was going to drag his son out of that bar and then finish with me. He claimed that my career was over. He left. I went home and brooded for several hours. I knew what I had to do. Al Meade needed to be stopped. I didn't know if he'd gone home so I decided to try the bar first. I went there and found him. We went into the alley, but it was too cold to stay outside. We talked in the Federal Building. The security system for the judges is a joke. I shot him when he went to the john. The tile was easy enough to clean. I wrapped the body up and took it downstairs in our private elevator. I thought I'd try and make it look like he was the closet case, so I tried to get the body into the dumpster behind Au Naturel. I was in a hurry and petrified about being caught. When the blood started to drip while I was carrying him, I stuck him in the next dumpster I came to."

"You knew Mike danced there," Turner said, "didn't you think the body being there would implicate him?"

Wadsworth shrugged then asked, "How did you find out he danced there?"

"He'd taken one of the guys to his place in Rogers Park to trick with him."

"Only the one?"

Turner nodded.

"Then, if not for that odd chance that the guy he went home with still worked there, you'd have never found out he was a dancer."

"Maybe not."

Fenwick said, "What happened with Mike?"

"I didn't see him until two nights later. He was impossible to get to talk to. Finally I got through. He agreed to meet at his place in Rogers Park. I didn't even know about it. When I went to get groceries this morning, I stopped in. I made a mistake. I thought he'd be happy that his dad was dead. Mike said he was going to go public about his sexuality. He said that his dad hurt lots of people and the only way he could see to make peace with himself was to tell all. He had already set up an interview with one of the national gay magazines. I was worried that any revelation on his part would reflect on me. He got angry at that. He said it was the closet and secrets that hurt. I told him I had freed us, and there was no need for public disclosure. I overestimated his affection for me.

"When I confessed what I had done, he was already overwhelmed by guilt. He told me he was going to tell the whole truth. He said hate and lying were what killed people. He was determined to stop this closeted crap, that this hiding in the closet had cost too much. He said he was never going to hide in the closet again. I couldn't let him get away with that. My life would be in ashes. You were never going to solve Judge Meade's murder. You all came to the conclusion that he was a closet case. You were wrong, of course, but it fit my purposes. None of this could come out. So I killed him."

"How'd you happen to have your gun with you when you went to see Mike?"

"Mike was the only one who knew I'd seen the judge the night before. On the phone, he'd mentioned going public with his life. This might have meant ruin to me. Certainly it would have ended our relationship. I wanted to convince him it wasn't that bad to hide, that we could have our lives together. I'd done it all these years and that, now that his dad was out of the way, things could go back to the way they were. He said he was going to tell. I had no choice. When he saw the gun, he tried to get away. I was between him and the door to the apartment. I guess he wanted to lock himself in the bathroom. I burst in before he even got the door closed. He shoved me and I fired. That's when I must have fallen. I bumped the radiator didn't I?" He looked at them. Their faces remained impassive. Wadsworth shrugged. "I shot him. I came here tonight because I realized the rolodex here was incriminating. I was too late."

"Premeditated murder, your honor," Fenwick said. "You were protecting your own butt."

"You don't understand."

"More than you imagine," Turner said.

An hour or so later two uniformed cops took the judge away. Turner and Fenwick stood in the hallway of the judge's home.

"You okay?" Fenwick asked.

"I don't like arresting people when I understand all too well what they've gone through."

"When you were coming out, you didn't murder anybody."

"Sometimes in high school I thought about killing myself."

Fenwick looked at him very carefully. "Being a gay kid can be tough. You've told me."

"I know. I think back on then, and wonder how I ever could have thought about it. I've got Jeff, and Brian, and Ben. Good friends, Mrs. Talucci, you, Ian. Back then there were times when it wasn't so good."

"Didn't your buddy Ian say that the vast majority of gay people thought about suicide at some time?"

"Yeah. I guess. I don't know if he's right or not. All I know is about me and how much it hurt being a frightened gay kid. And I know now, more than ever, that closets can kill. Let's get the hell out of here."

Paul didn't get home until six the next morning. Jeff was still asleep. Ben was at the kitchen table drinking coffee. He wore only his pajama bottoms. Paul admired his well-muscled and hirsute chest.

"You up all night?" Paul asked.

"No. I woke up early and you weren't here. I couldn't find anything else in the house to read so I picked up one of Jeff's books." He held up *Freddy and the Men from Mars.* "Mostly, I was practicing not worrying. After Jeff woke up, I was going to go over and see Rose Talucci."

Turner got a container of orange juice out of the refrigerator and poured himself a glass. He sat across from Ben.

"You okay?" Ben asked.

Turner told him what happened.

"That's tough on you," Ben said when he finished.

"None of those killings should have happened," Paul said. "They were gay and they were frightened, and now people are dead because of it. That's all it is."

They met Brian's plane at the airport late Sunday evening. He was beautifully tanned and nauseatingly cheerful. Brian put down his heaps of packages, shook Ben's hand, hugged his little brother, and wrapped an arm around his dad's shoulder. He grabbed several of his bundles. He passed one to Jeff who put it in his lap in the wheelchair and tore off the cover. It was a football signed by all the members of the Miami Dolphins.

"How'd you get this?" Jeff asked.

"I paid for it like anybody else. I got you guys something too," he said. He grinned at his dad and Ben. He held out two bulky packages to them. "I was thinking of getting you matching rhinestone-studded leather jockstraps from Key West, but I got you these instead." Turner looked inside the large bags. Two pink flamingoes.

Jeff tugged at the bags. "Lemme see."

Paul handed the birds to Jeff, then hugged his older son.